The Secret Library

Essential sensual reading

More great titles in
The Secret Library

Traded Innocence
9781908262028

Silk Stockings
9781908262042

The Thousand and One Nights
9781908262080

The Game
9781908262103

Hungarian Rhapsody
9781908262127

Masquerade

3 sensual novellas

Masquerade
by Elizabeth Coldwell

Seducing Mr Storm
by Poppy Summers

Freefalling
by Zara Stoneley

Published by Xcite Books Ltd – 2013
ISBN 9781908766137

Masquerade
Copyright © Elizabeth Coldwell 2013

Seducing Mr Storm
Copyright © Poppy Summers 2013

Freefalling
Copyright © Zara Stoneley 2013

The right of Elizabeth Coldwell, Poppy Summers and Zara Stoneley to be identified as the authors of this work has been asserted by them in accordance with the Copyright, Designs and Patents Act 1988

The stories contained within this book are works of fiction. Names and characters are the product of the authors' imaginations and any resemblance to actual persons, living or dead, is entirely coincidental.

All rights reserved. No part of this book may be reproduced, stored in a retrieval system, or transmitted in any form or by any means, electronic, electrostatic, magnetic tape, mechanical, photocopying, recording or otherwise, without the written permission of the publishers: Xcite Books, Suite 11769, 2nd Floor, 145-157 St John Street, London EC1V 4PY

Cover design by Madamadari

Masquerade by Elizabeth Coldwell

Let go from her sales job, Summer Kerrigan finds new employment at her local bar. It's nothing like her old routine, but there's welcome compensation in the shape of her cute boss, Eddie Quinn. When Eddie's sister, businesswoman Heather, turns up at the bar selling tickets for the fundraising Masquerade Ball, he claims Summer's his new love. But if Heather's going to buy the lie they're really a couple, they have to attend the ball as a couple – and with champagne flowing, passions run high, and Eddie and Summer find themselves in bed together. The sex is mind-blowing, but is it simply the result of taking part in a charade? Can their sham love affair turn into the real thing, or is it all just a masquerade?

Seducing Mr Storm by Poppy Summers

In the late 1700s, Susanna Seymour's mother is very keen to find a husband for her younger sister, Lucy, while Susanna is considered on the shelf at 27. Enter their neighbour arrived from London, the dashing and irreverent Elijah Storm, who makes his admiration plain for Susanna from the start. Susanna is not looking for a husband and is keen to make sure Lucy bags the bachelor, but things don't go quite to plan. Elijah is frank in his desire to have Susanna's sexual services, and she believes by giving him what he wants, he will lose all interest in her. The price of it is his agreement to marry her sister. But with passions ignited, what will happen when Susanna seduces Mr Storm?

Freefalling by Zara Stoneley

Falling in love has just been scrubbed off artist Hayley Tring's to-do list. But when the gorgeous Tom Holah commissions a painting, keeping her mind on the job and her hand on a paintbrush becomes a whole new challenge. Tom needs to brighten up his corporate image, but after a lust-filled night with Hayley he wants more than just her pictures. And he isn't used to taking no for an answer. But can mixing business with pleasure be good for both of them? Or will it leave Hayley with a blank canvas and a broken heart?

Contents

Masquerade 1
Seducing Mr Storm 75
Freefalling 149

Masquerade
by Elizabeth Coldwell

Chapter One

WHEN THE BOSS CALLED me into her office, I thought she was going to tell me off for staring at Calvin Blake's ass again. Frankly, I wanted to tell her, it would have been rude of me not to. Calvin might have been everything I disliked in a man – loud, brash, and self-serving, all personality traits that made him ideal for his job in ad sales but would have had me bailing on him in minutes if we'd been out on a date – but his behind was a force of nature. Sculpted into taut, round perfection by his regular lunchtime workouts, it was caressed by his slate-grey slacks as he bent over the desk next to mine, drawing my eye away from my computer monitor. I stared for a good couple of minutes; I may even have drooled a little. Only Mary Lou's nasal voice in my ear dragged me back to awareness that I was sitting in the middle of a busy sales floor, rather than some intimate boudoir where I could strip Calvin of his lower garments and admire those buns of steel in the raw, before landing a hard, satisfying slap against his bare, white flesh ...

'Hey, Summer, are you even listening to me? I said Rebecca needs to see you right away.'

Rebecca Haynes's PA, Mary Lou, always breezed into

the sales department with the confidence of somebody who knew she didn't have much in the way of power, but could use the little she possessed to make your life considerably more miserable. The thin smile on her over-glossed lips didn't reach her eyes. It never did.

'Yeah, sure, Mary Lou. Be right with you.' I clicked my mouse, closing down the spreadsheet whose figures I'd been updating before Calvin's ass had provided such a welcome distraction. Then I followed her across the floor to Rebecca's corner office. No one looked up as I passed, all too busy chasing the sale that would help fill the remaining couple of pages in tomorrow's *Reporter*.

Rebecca was on the phone as I entered, gesturing to me to take a seat. I did so, admiring as always the panorama of Lower Manhattan, revealed through the floor-to-ceiling window. Tall fingers of steel and glass pointed up toward the sky, glittering in the afternoon sun, each one higher and more imposing than the next. The more important you were in any company, the better the view you had, though I sometimes wondered quite how much time Rebecca spent appreciating this magnificent skyline.

At last, she put the phone down and turned her attention to me. If Mary Lou's smile had been cold, the one greeting me now was positively glacial. Rebecca Haynes and I had never had any time for each other. She thought I was a slacker who could find a thousand ways of filling her day before even thinking about attempting to sell any ad space, and I thought she was a flint-hearted bitch, only interested in the bottom line. In the past, she'd expressed her displeasure at everything from the blood-red streaks in my dark hair to my occasionally erratic timekeeping. I always promised that things would change, and for a while they did, though I never went so far as to get rid of the streaks. I loved them too much.

Another boss might have attempted some small talk, maybe even offered me a coffee, but not Rebecca. She cut straight to the chase.

'As you know, Summer, these are tough times for the *New York Reporter*.' Of course I did. Rebecca sent out a memo to this effect at least one a week, exhorting us all to work harder and help claw back some market share. 'We've seen our print sales fall by nearly 20 per cent over the last six months. Of course, our online version has tripled its number of hits in the same period, but that isn't really making up for the shortfall in revenue. So, we've had to make some tough decisions, particularly regarding staffing levels … And I'm afraid we're going to have to let you go.'

How had I not seen this coming? I knew I'd missed my sales targets the last couple of months, but I'd never dreamt this was putting me at risk of losing my job. Would I have worked harder, kissed more corporate ass if I had? I honestly didn't know.

'I'm sure you'll find the severance package you've been awarded very generous,' Rebecca continued as I sat in silent shock, trying to take in what she'd just told me. 'And you'll have a few minutes to clear your desk …'

Somehow, I found my voice. 'You mean you want me to leave now?'

'Of course, Summer. What else did you think? That we'd let you stick around long enough to poach our client list, maybe sneak some virus into the computer system? Please …' Behind me, the office door opened. When I looked round, Mary Lou stood in the doorway, that same unfriendly smile on her face, a sturdy brown cardboard box in her hand. Alongside her was Tim, one of the company's security guards. It always seemed to me he'd been hired for his charming manner on the front desk rather than as serious muscle, seeing as how he stood barely any taller than my own five foot five, and looked swamped by his navy blue serge uniform.

Even though I knew this was standard procedure, it didn't make me feel any better as the guy escorted me to my desk and stood watching as I started packing my few personal possessions, just to make sure I didn't try any clever ideas like downloading files on to a flash drive, or forwarding any confidential information to my personal email address.

Everyone had noticed what was going on, heads poking over the top of their cubicles like a mob of curious meerkats, but only Delia came over to say anything. Delia, my best friend in the company – hell, probably my best friend anywhere.

'Summer, what's happening?' she asked, a startled look on her pretty, heart-shaped face.

'Company cost-cutting,' I told her, 'and the cost they've decided to cut is me.'

'But that's just awful. You've been here – what, five years? Whatever happened to last in, first out?'

I shrugged. That might have been an effective policy, if it hadn't been for the fact almost all of the people who'd joined the department after me had already been promoted at least a grade higher. When I'd started here, I'd been at the bottom of the pile, and even after all this time, though I'd never intended it, that's where I'd managed to stay.

Delia laid her slender fingers over mine, and gave them a reassuring squeeze, letting me know everything would be OK, even if it didn't feel like it right now. 'What will you do?' she asked.

I hadn't even thought about it. 'I don't know. Go home. Cry. Punch the wall. Play Bon Jovi so loud the neighbours complain.'

'Well, at least you haven't lost your sense of humour, honey.' Delia grinned. She glanced round the floor. The initial excitement over, people were beginning to return to their work. 'Tell you what, when the dust's settled, we'll all go out and have a few drinks. Kind of like a belated leaving party. What do you say?'

'Maybe.' Apart from Delia, I didn't want to see any of my co-workers again once I walked out of here for good, not even to take a last, fond peek at Calvin's ass. Not able to bring myself to tell her that, I finished my packing.

The last of my things stowed in the cardboard box, I made to log off my computer, but Tim shook his head, warning me not to touch it. Instead, I gave Delia a quick hug, promising her I'd ring her very soon, and made my way to the elevator.

Tim and I rode down 32 floors in silence. It seemed like he didn't quite know what to say to me, and I wondered whether I was the first employee he'd ever had to escort from the premises. The way Rebecca had been talking, I guessed if sales of the *Reporter* didn't pick up soon, I wouldn't be the last. God help the guy if he ever needed to make sure the likes of big, athletic Calvin left the building without making a scene.

Only when we were outside on the sidewalk, my company identity pass clutched securely in his meaty fist, did he wish me luck. 'Thanks, Tim, take care of yourself,' I said, and stood watching till he'd disappeared back inside through the revolving doors of a building in which I no longer worked.

The warmth of the spring air was like a caress on my skin, with none of the oppressive humidity that could make being outside in high summer so uncomfortable. Rather than take the subway back to my apartment, I decided to walk the 20-odd blocks. I needed to clear my head, try and make sense of what had just happened to me. And like I'd told Delia, when I got home maybe I'd just have a darn good cry.

Or maybe I'd get roaring drunk. That thought popped into my head a block from home, as I passed the bar on the corner, Eddie's. In all the time I'd lived in the Village, I'd never been inside. Somehow, I'd managed to gain the impression the place was a dive, somewhere guys hung out to watch sports and discuss their most recent bedroom conquest. If I went out with Delia and the girls from work, we tended to frequent the latest upscale cocktail joint that had been featured in the *Reporter*'s pages, somewhere Wall Street types hung out. Delia harboured fantasies of marrying a man with money, but only ever succeeded in meeting jerks. She hadn't yet learnt the two things so often went hand in hand.

Yes, I decided, I'd have a drink or two; enough to soften the blow of getting laid off, not enough to get maudlin. Though the more I analysed it, the more I realised self-pity wasn't high on the list of emotions I was feeling right now. Indeed, if I'd been in Rebecca's position, needing to lose a staff member, I'd have picked myself as the one who should go. I'd never been cut out for a career in sales, not really; when I'd left college, I hadn't had a clue what I wanted to do with the rest of my life, so I'd sent out a bunch of résumés, responding to any advert that had taken my interest. A friend of a friend had happened to mention there was a vacancy in the *New York Reporter*'s ad sales department, so I fired off a quick application and a week later, after an interview where I'd convincingly managed to overstate my credentials, I'd landed the job. I only wished I hadn't gone on to lose it at the point the economy had gone into freefall. It wouldn't be so easy to bluff my way into employment a second time round. If I wasn't careful, I might begin with all the right intentions – updating my résumé and sending it to only the most reputable employment agencies – but soon find myself reduced to scanning the adverts on Craigslist for any part-time and seasonal work that didn't require me to take my top off.

Just as I was about to push open the door and go inside, a hand appeared in the bar's mullioned front window. It clutched a large sheet of white paper, with something printed on it. A second hand joined the first, and pressed the notice firmly to the glass, adhesive tape securing it in place. In bold block capitals, the sign read "BARMAID WANTED. APPLY WITHIN".

It felt like a message from above. On my walk down from the *Reporter* office, mulling over my options – or lack of them – in my mind, I'd never considered working in a bar. It kind of seemed like a good few steps down from my cosy office job. But now, thinking about the bills that were due at the end of the month, and the rent on my apartment that no severance package, however generous, could cover indefinitely, it might turn out to be the perfect solution, at least on a short-term basis. The notice hadn't specified that experience was necessary, which helped, as I didn't have any. But working in a bar meant taking orders, fetching drinks, smiling, and being nice to people, and I could do that. Taking a deep breath to steady myself, I walked into the bar.

It being the middle of the afternoon, the place was quiet; only a couple of guys propping up the bar and what I took to be a pair of middle-aged tourists sitting in a booth, if the guide book resting on the table between them was any reliable indication. The place felt a little run down, with its battered wooden booths, and fly-spotted glass-shaded lights hanging from the ceiling, but in a good way, as though the memories of a thousand nights spent in the company of good friends and sociable strangers had leached into the walls and floorboards.

'Hey, what can I get you?' the bartender asked as I approached.

My confident intended reply died in my throat. I could only stare at the guy who'd addressed me. Whatever I'd been expecting the owner of the want ad-clutching hands to look like, it wasn't this combination of height and breadth, shaggy dark hair and scruffily bearded chin that had me taking an awestruck breath. The T-shirt he wore, emblazoned with the bar's logo, stretched tight across his chest, like he might burst out of it at any moment. When he smiled, the creases at the corners of his hazel eyes crinkling, my insides seemed to turn to warm syrup, and my pussy clenched with need. It took me a little while to collect myself enough to speak.

'I'm here about the barmaid job,' I told him, glad the tears that had threatened to come as I'd cleared my desk hadn't tumbled down my cheeks to ruin my make-up.

He gave a soft whistle. 'Wow, that was fast. I only just this minute put the sign up.'

'Well, I happened to be passing, and I hate to let an opportunity slip by,' I offered by way of explanation. 'Who do I need to speak to?'

'That would be me. Eddie Quinn. I own this place.' He held out a big paw of a hand for me to shake. I did so a little awkwardly, cradling the box containing everything I'd brought from my desk at the *Reporter* in the crook of my arms. The fuzzy leaves of the purple passion plant I'd received as a present from Delia the previous Christmas drooped forlornly over its rim.

'Summer Kerrigan,' I replied, feeling a sudden tingling

as his skin touched mine. The sweetness of the contact reminded me of how long it had been since my last relationship had ended. I'd met Todd on a girls' night out with Delia. We'd had one of those three-week flings that burns hot as fire at the start, then fizzles out as soon as you realise you have nothing in common outside the bedroom. Nice as it had been, I wasn't looking for any more of the same. Next time, I wanted to meet someone who was in it for the long haul; someone who shared the same goals in life as I did. Though what those goals were, I wasn't exactly sure any more, not now my former career path had so unexpectedly come to an end. Which reminded me of why I was standing here, still feeling the subtle pressure of Eddie's hand against my own even though we'd long since broken the physical contact.

I couldn't help noticing Eddie's gaze had moved from the box I held. It took a slow up and down trail of my body, appraising me; assessing me, I hoped, as a suitable employee. Unless he was just checking me out, of course.

'So, Summer, have you got any experience of working in a bar?'

I shook my head. Honesty had to be the best policy, even if it meant I didn't get the job. 'I don't, and I'm afraid I don't have an up-to-date résumé with me either. I wasn't exactly intending to put myself up for a job interview this afternoon. But I'm enthusiastic, I learn fast, and I literally only live round the corner.' What more could I tell him?

He regarded me with the expression of a man not entirely convinced by my sales pitch. 'I'm looking for someone who's prepared to work shifts, and I'm not talking nine to five. You might not finish here till two in the morning.'

'Not a problem,' I assured him. I'd always been a night

bird; it was the reason I'd slept through my alarm on more than one occasion, earning Rebecca's wrath when I eventually made it into the office.

'OK, well, I pay nine bucks an hour.' Eddie spoke almost as though he was laying down a challenge, waiting for me to back down and admit I wasn't cut out for the job. When I just kept looking at him, waiting for him to tell me something I couldn't cope with, he added, 'Though you can push that up with tips, of course.'

'Of course.' I'd be a fool to deny the money wasn't a significant drop in salary compared to what I'd been used to, but I'd manage. It wouldn't hurt to cut down on a few of my extravagances, resisting the urge to buy new shoes I really didn't need. I couldn't say why I suddenly wanted this job so badly, but it had plenty to do with the prospect of working alongside this brawny, sleepy-eyed bartender.

'What T-shirt size are you?' Eddie asked. 'Small?'

It seemed like a pretty personal question from someone I'd only just met. 'Why d'you ask?'

'Well, the staff uniform involves one of these –' he gestured to the T-shirt he wore '– and your choice of pants or a skirt, though wearing a skirt'll always earn you more in the way of tips. Especially with legs like yours.'

So he had been checking me out, though I couldn't complain. After all, I'd been doing exactly the same to him. It took me a moment to realise the real significance of his comment.

'You mean I've got the job?' I would have hugged him, but that would mean putting the box down, and where we stood there wasn't anywhere to do that apart from the floor. 'Oh, thanks so much, Eddie. I promise you, you won't regret this.'

The look he gave me indicated he wasn't so sure about that. All he said was, 'I'll need you here at five tomorrow afternoon. Don't be late.'

With that remark, I'd gone from laid-off salesperson to the newest barmaid at Eddie's on Barrow Street in the space of little more than an hour. It wasn't the career move I'd intended to take, and I told myself I wasn't being guided in my decision purely by an attack of lust for my new boss. I'd never mixed business with pleasure, and I wasn't going to start now, however cute the man might be. But as I stepped back out on to the street, I swore I could still feel the touch of his hand, branded on my skin, and I knew if nothing else my dreams that night would be very sweet indeed.

Chapter Two

THE ALARM WENT OFF the next morning at seven, just as it always did. I almost dragged myself out of bed and headed for the bathroom, until I remembered I didn't work at the *Reporter* any more. I could kiss goodbye to my old routine. No shower in water that would more than likely be lukewarm, thanks to the indifferent plumbing in this old apartment block; no breakfast on the run; no squeezing myself on to a packed and sweaty subway train for the ride to Times Square. Eddie didn't need me for my first shift at the bar until five that night. For pretty much the first time since I'd graduated from college, the whole day was my own.

Rolling over, I drifted off to sleep again. Though my plan to have a drink or two at Eddie's had been derailed by my impromptu job interview, I'd stopped off at the local liquor store on the way back to my apartment and picked up a bottle of Prosecco. I'd toasted the end of my old career and the start of my new one, finishing off most of the bottle in the process. When I'd finally made it to bed around midnight, my dreams had been a confused jumble, though I clearly remembered that at one point I'd dreamt of Eddie and me standing in the middle of his bar room, sharing a long, slow, sensuous kiss.

When I woke for a second time, it was almost ten. This, I knew, was going to be the pattern of my days from now on: sleeping late; eating a leisurely breakfast; maybe taking long walks round the neighbourhood, getting to know it better than I had at any time since I'd moved here.

Not bothering to dress, I went into the kitchen to brew myself a pot of coffee. Looking in the fridge, I noticed I was low on milk and a few of the other essentials. Once I'd had breakfast, I'd go out and pick up some groceries, and drop off a couple of items to be dry cleaned. Maybe I'd even start going through my wardrobe, picking out stuff I didn't wear any more to take to one of the local thrift stores. At last I had time to do all the chores I'd been putting off.

Waiting for the kettle to boil, I couldn't help wondering what Delia would be doing right about now. Probably stuck in some boring meeting, or on a client call. I'd sent her a text message last night, telling her I'd found myself a new job. She'd sent me a brief "congratulations" in response. I resisted the urge to check in and give her all the details; Rebecca frowned on anyone making personal calls or sending non-business emails on company time, and I didn't want to get my best friend into any trouble, not with things on the newspaper the way they were.

Coffee brewed, I poured myself a mug and stood staring out of the window as I sipped it. I didn't have the greatest view in the city, nothing like the one from Rebecca Haynes's office. All I could see was the rear of the building that backed on to mine, a dull red brick affair dominated by a rickety iron fire escape. I'd never paid it that much attention, but now I realised there were two people standing on it, locked in a passionate clinch.

The sight was so unexpected, I couldn't help but stare at it. I knew the day had a different rhythm for those who didn't work the usual office hours, but I'd never imagined people might pass their time with such an open display of public affection, and in such a precarious location too.

They broke the kiss so they could stare into each other's eyes, and I got a better look at the two of them. Looking young enough to be a student from NYU, he was tall and lanky, bare-chested in the morning sunshine. A blackwork tattoo swirled around most of the length of his right arm. The girl with him was reaching for the fly of his jeans, tugging it open. She had on a floral dress that buttoned down the front; it had already been opened halfway, and though her curtain of long, blonde hair all but covered her breasts, when she moved it was pretty easy to tell she didn't have a bra on beneath it. As her companion worked on the rest of the buttons, I caught the briefest flash of fur-covered pussy and realised she wasn't wearing panties either.

That's the point when I should have stepped away from the window, and left them to their private moment. It was pretty obvious where this scene was headed, after all. But I figured it couldn't be that private, if they'd stepped out on to the fire escape to fuck. Maybe they'd done so in the hope that someone would be staring out of a neighbouring window, watching as the guy bent his head, pushing the girl's hair and the open flap of her dress front out of the way so he could suck on her tit.

Just watching them, I felt myself start to get wet, pussy lips blooming against the thin cotton of my pyjama bottoms. It was hardly surprising, given the show in front of me. The couple was young, attractive and, judging by their body language, more in lust than in love. Just like Todd and I had been. Though we'd never been so bold as to take our lovemaking out of the bedroom – apart from one memorable occasion where he'd fucked me on the kitchen table of his apartment in Brooklyn Heights.

The girl had her head thrown back, pleasure etched on

her face, as her lover's mouth trailed down the valley between her breasts, kissing and nipping. Slowly but purposefully he moved closer to her bare pussy. Setting down the coffee mug, my hand slipped beneath the waistband of my pyjamas as I continued to watch them, fingers encountering sticky wetness when I traced them along my cleft. I'd never thought of myself as a voyeur – an ex of mine had once suggested we watch a porno together, and I'd got bored after less than 20 minutes, more interested in the horny, flesh-and-blood guy on the sofa at my side than the buff but strangely plastic-looking ones on the screen. Seeing the couple on the fire escape enjoying each other's bodies, oblivious to all around them, was affecting me powerfully, however. Almost without thinking, I stroked the hidden nub of my clit.

His head was level with the fork of her legs now, and though I couldn't see it, I knew his lips and tongue would be working on her pussy, parting the wet, velvet lips to seek out the treasures waiting within. She was clutching the iron rail of the fire escape with one hand, and squeezing and rolling one of her nipples with the other. I could only imagine the delicious sensations she must be feeling, jolts of pleasure from her sweetly tormented tit surging down to link with the rhythmic pulsing in her cunt.

Closing my eyes, I imagined myself getting some of the same expert treatment, a wet, supple tongue slithering over my pussy, licking me all the way from my clit to the tightly furled bud of my asshole. At first, I pictured the tattooed, shirtless guy crouching between my legs, eager to please, wanting to make sure he hit all the right spots as he pushed me toward orgasm. But cute as he might be, he wasn't my type – too young, and a little on the skinny side for my liking. So I replaced him with the man I really wanted down there, eating me out. Eddie Quinn. I couldn't remember the last time someone had elbowed their way to the front of my fantasy queue so quickly, but he'd managed it, even though I shouldn't be having such naughty thoughts about him, given we'd be working alongside each other from now on. Those concerns were easy to brush aside in the heat of the moment, though, and I went back to daydreaming about him. I knew he'd have a hard, muscular body beneath the T-shirt he'd had on yesterday, with wide shoulders I could grip on to as his mouth went to work on me. And as his tongue squirmed its way up into my channel, I'd sigh and hold him tighter, demanding more …

Forcing my attention back to the couple outside, in need of more fuel for my fantasy, I noticed they'd changed position. The guy now stood side on to the grimy brick wall, and his girlfriend had his cock in her hand. I didn't have as good a view of it as I'd like, but I could tell from the length of his shuttling strokes up and down his shaft that he was big. Forgetting my own pleasure, I craned my head, trying to get a better look. I still wasn't sure whether they had any clue I was watching, or if they were simply swept away by their own need for each other.

The blonde climbed up on to the bottom rung of the iron steps leading up to the next floor. They exchanged a few words which I couldn't make out – I wanted to open the window, but I knew the movement would alert them to the fact they had an audience who might, after all, not be so welcome. From his delighted grin and her wanton expression, though, I worked out she'd told him she was ready to be fucked. With her standing just a little higher than him, she was perfectly placed to guide the head of that long, thick cock into her hole. With a couple of jerking motions, he buried himself deep in her, her face registering the sheer delight of being joined to him in such intimate fashion. Then he began to thrust, hard and fast. Her hands clutched at his ass, urging him further inside, and her hair was whipped around her face by the breeze.

The fire escapes on these old buildings might be sturdier than they looked, but he was giving her such a pounding I really believed they might pry the structure loose from the bolts holding it to the wall. Captivated by the live sex show taking place outside my window, I returned to rubbing my clit, with more purpose this time. All fantasies forgotten, I used their fast, remorseless fucking, and the sight of his bare ass cheeks flexing in his lover's grasp with every stroke, to spur me on. It couldn't be long, I was sure, before one or other of them came, and I wanted an orgasm of my own, to match theirs.

He stepped up the pace, hips thrusting wildly. I was all wetness and need, slipping a finger into my hot, slick depths in a vain attempt to satisfy the craving I felt. My vibrator lay on the nightstand, but I feared by the time I returned from fetching it they'd have finished and gone. So two fingers of my right hand sufficed instead, pushing in and out of me while the middle finger of my left paid loving attention to my clit.

It was obvious to me they'd reached the final act of their performance. His thrusting had lost its steady pace; now he was urgent, uncontrolled, racing to the finish line. When he stilled, the straining of every sinew evident in his posture, I knew he'd come. My own orgasm hit me at roughly the same time as his girlfriend yelled something – curse words, his name, maybe even "I love you" – and surrendered to her pleasure. Gasping, knees buckling, I clutched on to the cold metal edge of the sink for support.

It took a moment for me to recover my composure. When I had, I looked out of the window to see the guy easing his jeans back up his tanned legs and the blonde buttoning her dress. The show was over.

A pang of envy consumed me as I watched the couple scurry down the fire escape, disappearing out of my line of vision. It wasn't so much because of their obvious enjoyment of each other, and sex, reminding of what I lacked in my own life. More it was their wildness, their lack of inhibition. Maybe with the right person, I could find something of that same spontaneity. Whoever that right person might be.

I took their brazen display as another indicator that the time was right to start making changes in my life, changes in myself. Working at Eddie's, I didn't need to be a corporate drone any more. Picking up my forgotten coffee mug, I wrinkled my nose as I took a sip of liquid that had gone cold. I'd have a shower, then brew myself a fresh pot. Think positive, Summer, I told myself, and this will all work out.

Pushing open the door of Eddie's just before five that night, I didn't feel quite so optimistic. Starting any new job is always nerve-racking, and I knew I'd have a lot to learn in a short time to make sure my lack of experience didn't find a way of biting me in the ass. The bar room was busier than it had been the day before, but Eddie paused in the act of pouring a beer and greeted me with a smile as I walked in.

I'd taken his advice, teaming my black uniform T-shirt with a denim skirt short enough to show off my thighs, but not so short that I'd be flashing my underwear every time I leant over a table.

'Hey, Summer, great to see you.' Eddie motioned over the barmaid who was wiping down the table in one of the booths. 'Summer, meet Janeane. She tends to work the early shifts here, but I'll warn you now you might have to step in to cover for her if one of her kids is sick.'

'Oh, do you have boys or girls?' I asked, as Janeane gave me a broad smile that caused the creases in the corners of her eyes to deepen.

'One of each,' she said, pushing a stray lock of dyed blonde hair behind her ear. 'Molly's six and Mikey's three, and they're a real handful between them. But I wouldn't be without them, believe me.'

'Hey, waitress!' a voice called behind her.

She turned to see who needed attention, with a quick "Catch you later" in my direction.

'Janeane goes off shift at six,' Eddie told me, 'and Sunday to Thursday you'll be working on your own when she leaves. Friday and Saturday, there'll be two of you, but you'll meet Penny in due course. Now come on, let me give you a quick tour of the place.'

He came out from behind the bar. Again, I was struck by his sheer physical size; he towered over me, and would have done even if I hadn't been wearing the flat shoes I knew would be most comfortable for spending all night on my feet. My mind flashed back to the couple on the fire escape, and I wondered how many rungs I'd have to climb to be on a level with Eddie's crotch as he guided his cock into me. That image I quickly brushed away; it didn't do to be thinking about my new boss in those terms, even though he was so close to me I could smell the subtle, masculine scent of him. He didn't appear to favour cologne, unlike the guys in the *Reporter* office, who between them had smelled like the perfume counter at Bloomingdale's. I felt like I could stand there just breathing him in for ever, but instead I was ushered through to the small back kitchen to meet Rudy, the bar's short order cook.

Rudy turned out to be short and stocky, with a blue-striped, grease-spotted apron tied round his waist and a black bandanna keeping his greying hair out of his eyes. The aura he gave off was that of a man in charge of his own domain. He thrust out a hand for me to shake as Eddie again made introductions.

'Nice to meet you, Summer. You're going to love working here,' he said, before returning to tend to the burgers sizzling on the hot plate. The menu at Eddie's, which was chalked up on a board on the wall by the bar, tended toward the basic – burgers, fries, hot wings, Philly cheese steaks; the ideal accompaniment to a pitcher of beer and a football game on TV – but Rudy's cooking looked deliciously appetising.

Almost before I knew it, Eddie had handed me an apron with pockets for the notepad and pen I'd use for writing down orders, and the cash I'd be taking in payment. I fastened it around my waist, and went to serve my first customer.

That first night passed in a blur, as I got to grips with the process of taking orders for food and drink, delivering them to Eddie or Rudy as required, and then bringing everything back to the customers. Eddie's attracted a mixed crowd – students, sports fans, off-duty firefighters from the firehouse over on West 10th Street – and though it wasn't as busy as it would get on Friday and Saturday nights, the atmosphere was convivial and pleasantly noisy. The jukebox had been loaded up with rock classics, mostly from the 70s and 80s, and a TV over the bar showed the local news channel with the sound turned way down. Eddie commanded the area behind the bar, pouring beer from the dozen or so taps; mostly microbrews, many of them from the renowned Brooklyn Brewery, just over the other side of the Hudson. No fancy mixed drinks or flinging cocktail shakers in the air with a flourish for him.

By the end of the night my feet ached, even in spite of my comfortable shoes, and I had to stifle a yawn or two as we closed up the bar. But I couldn't deny I'd had fun; striking up a rapport with the customers had been much easier than trying to persuade a reluctant client to buy more columns of ad space, and I'd had more than a few admiring glances as I'd passed between tables with my tray. If men wanted to flirt, I was happy to flirt back; most of the time, it meant an extra dollar or two to add to the tip jar Eddie kept in the kitchen, the contents of which, he'd told me, were divided up between the wait staff and Rudy at the end of the week. And they could chat to me all they wanted, passing me their numbers scribbled on napkins when they handed me their money; it wasn't like I was going to take any of them up on their offers.

It could just have been my imagination, but a couple of times I swore I could see Eddie looking my way too, his expression giving the impression he liked what he saw. Then he'd quickly return to washing beer glasses, or whatever he'd been doing before. The thought of the craggily handsome bar owner paying me a little attention put a spring in my step, and broadened my smile, but I told myself not to make too much of it. Maybe he was just pleased I hadn't messed up any customer orders, or slipped and sent a plate of chicken wings smothered in Rudy's own-recipe hot sauce crashing to the ground.

'Goodnight, Summer,' Eddie said, as he let me out of the door. 'You did really well for your first night, you know.' His tone suggested he didn't regret taking me on, which I counted as an achievement.

'Thanks, it's been fun,' I replied, meaning it despite the blister forming on my left heel. Whatever I was about to add was cut off by the blare of a siren as a police car raced down the street.

'Are you going to be OK to get home?' Eddie seemed suddenly reminded that, despite the sustained attempts at cracking down on street crime, this city could still be a dangerous place, particularly late at night.

'Honestly, Eddie, I'll be fine. Like I said, I only live round the corner.'

'You're sure? I could walk you there, if you'd like.'

Such a tempting offer. On the doorstep, I could invite him in for coffee, and see what that might lead to. I'd dreamt of sharing a kiss with him; maybe tonight it would happen, then I'd lead him into the bedroom and …

I pulled myself up sharply. What was I thinking? I barely knew the guy. My usual rule specified three dates before I ended up in bed with someone; it didn't make me look too eager, and gave me time to ensure I really liked him enough to take things to the next stage. Tonight wasn't the time to do anything more than thank Eddie for his concern and assure him I was fine to make my way home alone. 'I'll see you tomorrow,' I said, and with that I was gone.

I looked back when I'd walked about a hundred yards, expecting to see nothing but a firmly locked door. Instead, Eddie still stood there. Giving him a wave that caused him to pop his head back inside, as though embarrassed I'd caught him watching me, I hurried on my way.

Chapter Three

AFTER A WEEK OR so, it felt like I'd never done anything but work at Eddie's. My time on the *Reporter* seemed like another life, grey and dull, and even though I'd taken a substantial hit in terms of salary, the camaraderie with my new colleagues helped to compensate. Plenty of things were more important than money, after all.

As I lingered over a second mug of strong coffee one morning, my cell phone rang. When I picked it up, I heard Eddie's voice. 'Hey, Summer, I need you to come in and work the lunch shift, if that's OK.'

'Sure,' I replied, glancing at my watch to make sure I had enough time to shower and change before the bar opened at 11. 'Is there some problem with Janeane?'

'Yeah, she's had to take Molly to the dentist's office. The kid's been up half the night with a raging toothache, apparently. I hate having to ask you to do this, but I rang Penny and she's in classes all morning.'

'Don't worry about it, honestly, Eddie. I'm happy to help out.'

The bar had a different vibe in the hour after opening. The scent of stale beer had been cleaned away, and the jukebox, programmed to choose random songs if no one was around to pay for their own selection, played Bruce Springsteen and the Eagles at a low volume.

Eddie, I couldn't help but notice, had a copy of that

day's *Reporter* on the bar, and was reading the latest on some new scandal engulfing the Mayor's office. 'Can you believe how corrupt people can be?' he commented to no one in particular. 'Show 'em a trough and next thing you know they've got their noses in it. What do you think, hey, Summer?'

'I think I could have gone a little longer without seeing that rag again.' I gestured to the paper. When he raised a quizzical eyebrow, I added, 'The day I came in here looking for a job, I'd just got laid off from the *Reporter*'s advertising department.'

The explanation made me realise how little Eddie and I knew about each other. We'd chatted as we worked, but mostly making small talk about the weather or the foibles of some customer or other, nothing of any consequence. With the bar so quiet, I took the opportunity to rectify that.

'So what about you? How long have you owned this place?'

Eddie folded the paper shut, and set it down on the counter top. 'A little over four years now. Before that, I was in construction. Did a lot of work around the Village, and a few of the guys used to drink here all the time. It was called the Barrow Tavern in those days, and it was a proper dive. Just real neglected, you know? And it's in such a prime location, I always thought with just a little investment, it could be a great little neighbourhood bar.' He broke off as a man walked up to the counter. 'Hey, Tyler, what can I get you?'

As the lanky, dark-haired guy Eddie had addressed as Tyler settled himself on a bar stool, I fought to suppress a grin. His black tank top left his arms bare, and the blackwork tattoo on his right arm was instantly familiar to me. The last time I'd seen it had been from my kitchen window as he clung on tight to his blonde lover, fucking her on the fire escape. Now here he was, thumbs pressing rapidly at the keypad of his cell phone while he waited for Eddie to pour his beer.

'You know him?' I asked, once he'd been served and Eddie turned his attention back to me.

'Oh, I know any number of people to say hi to,' Eddie replied. 'But yeah, Tyler's in here all the time. Though I'm surprised to see him on his own. He usually has some girl or other hanging off his arm. Very popular with the ladies, is Tyler.'

If what I'd been a witness to the other day was a typical performance, I had a good idea why. 'So,' I said, switching back to our original topic of conversation, 'you were telling me how you came to buy the bar?'

'Oh yeah. Well, it was always a dream of mine to own a bar, but I never saw it happening. I'd managed to put some savings aside, but nothing like as much as I'd need. Then I found out that my old man had put quite a large sum of money in trust for me, and once I turned 30 I could get my hands on it. Talk about fate, but a month after my 30th birthday, the owners put this place up for sale and – well, you can guess the rest.'

So if his father had put money in trust, did that mean the man was dead, or …? Rudy yelling, 'Order up!' from the kitchen put a halt to me asking any more questions, as I went to collect the burger and fries that had been ordered by the man in the booth closest to the door.

A party of tourists wandered in, commandeering my attention and embarking on a rambling, complicated order of food and drinks. As they were deciding whether they wanted their burgers with blue cheese and mushrooms or bacon and avocado, I looked over toward the bar and caught Eddie's eye. He winked, the action so unutterably sexy it sent a thrill of excitement skittering through me.

'Oh waitress, could I make that a large glass of white zinfandel?' the woman who'd been taking longest to make up her mind asked in a slow, southern drawl.

'Sure thing,' I said, scribbling her request on my pad. 'I'll be right back with the drinks.'

There was so much more I wanted to ask Eddie, but he appeared to be engrossed in conversation with Tyler, pointing to the same story in the *Reporter* he'd been discussing with me. There'd be time, I told myself, and went to take the food order through to Rudy.

A couple of nights later, another familiar face crossed the threshold of Eddie's. Delia had sent a couple of texts promising she'd come down and visit me, but I was still a little surprised to see her walk into the bar one Thursday evening. It was stormy outside, and she paused for a second in the doorway to shake her umbrella free of raindrops. I'd half-expected her to bring some of the girls from the *Reporter* with her, but she'd come on her own. She found a spare seat at the bar, perching on it daintily as she waited to be served.

'Hey, Summer, how's it going?' she asked as I walked past her carrying a tray of beers for a noisy bunch of Giants fans in the booth closest to the TV. They were regulars, rowdy but good-natured, and they tipped well, which had endeared them to me. Occasionally, they'd ask me how I thought the team would do, and I'd just shake my head and make a wild guess, knowing next to nothing about football.

'Hi, Delia. Welcome to Eddie's. Pretty filthy night outside, huh?'

'Yeah, whatever happened to the heat wave they were promising on the news?'

Eddie set down a round paper mat with a fluted edge in front of Delia, and placed a glass of red wine on it. At the side of it, he put the complimentary dish of mixed nuts he offered to all customers with their drink. 'Friend of yours, hey, Summer?'

'Yes, this is Delia. We used to work on the *Reporter* together.'

'Pleased to meet you, Delia. Any friend of Summer's is a friend of mine.' He seemed about to add something else, but noticed someone further down the bar indicating that he wanted another beer, and went to oblige.

Delia sipped her wine. 'So, it looks like you're doing OK.'

'Yeah, I'm enjoying it so much,' I assured her, the enthusiasm in my tone obvious even to my own ears. 'Eddie's a great boss to work for, and we get a really nice crowd in here.'

'And to think we always reckoned this place was full of sports nuts and losers.' Delia grinned. 'So what's all that about?' She gestured to one of the beer taps at the back of the bar, which was crowned by a photograph of a silver-haired, middle-aged man in a firefighter's uniform.

'What, Sergeant O'Malley's Ale?' I'd asked the same question on my first night at work, and Eddie had filled me in on the story. 'He used to drink in here when he was off shift, along with the rest of his crew, and that was his favourite tipple. He was killed rescuing a girl from a burning building on East 14th Street a couple of years back, and that's when Eddie decided to rename the beer in his honour.'

Delia raised her wine glass in the direction of the man's photograph, paying her own silent tribute to him. Like all New Yorkers, she appreciated the sacrifices the emergency services made in the course of keeping the city safe. Then she took a sip of her drink, and her eyes brightened. 'So what you're saying is the bar gets full of firefighters? Maybe I should start drinking here on a regular basis.'

'Whatever happened to your dream of hooking a rich stockbroker?' I asked, casting an eye round the bar room to make sure no one was in imminent need of serving.

'Oh, maybe what I really need is a guy who's more down to earth, got some dirt under his fingernails, you know?' She flashed me a secretive smile. 'Just like you've got here.'

'Delia, what are you talking about?' A noisy party of four in the back booth had stood up to leave, throwing a pile of dollar bills down on the table, and I had to go collect the money and clean away the empty glasses.

'Well, you can't deny your boss is hot, with that fine ass and that whole "just got out of bed" thing going on. You've landed on your feet here, Summer, really you have, and I'm just wondering what you're going to do about it?'

'Oh, you're crazy,' I told her, leaving her to her wine and nibbles while I attended to the recently vacated booth.

That didn't stop me thinking about her words even after she'd finished her drink and bid me goodnight – though not before filling me in on all the gossip from the *Reporter*, including the rumour that they were looking to make further job cuts, not only in the advertising department, but on the editorial floor too. She was pretty sure her own position was safe, but she admitted she'd started looking at online job listings, just in case.

Delia was smart, and good at what she did; I knew if the worst did happen, she'd find a similar position without too much difficulty. Still, it didn't stop me worrying about her a little.

The bar had closed for the night, and I had just pulled on a hooded top, ready to leave for my apartment and bed, when a tall, sharp-featured woman pushed through the door, carrying a furled umbrella.

'I'm sorry, we're closed,' I told her, but she ignored me and strode up to the counter.

She appeared to be looking round for something. Failing to find it, she finally acknowledged me. 'Where's Eddie?'

'Oh, he's in the back kitchen, I think. I'll go get him.'

'Don't bother,' she said, and walked round the side of the counter, into an area that was strictly off-limits to customers.

'Hey, you're not supposed to –' I began, wondering how to get her out of there, but at that moment Eddie emerged from the kitchen, his face breaking into a weary grin at the sight of the trespasser.

'Hey, sis, what brings you here?' Turning to me, he said, 'Summer, this is my sister, Heather.'

'Stepsister,' she corrected him. That explained why I couldn't see any strong physical similarities between them, and why Heather was as fair as her brother was dark. Cold and brusque where he was open and charming.

'Anyway, what brings you here at this time of night?' Eddie asked. I thought about leaving, but something in his tone compelled me to stay. There seemed to be a little frost around the edges of this sibling relationship, and I wondered whether he felt as though he needed a spot of back-up.

'The Masquerade Ball at the Mallory Hotel. You haven't forgotten, have you?'

From the blank look on Eddie's face, it was obvious he had.

'Oh Eddie. I must have reminded you three or four

times. It's this Saturday night, and you know I'm counting on you to be there.' Sensing Eddie was about to make some kind of objection, Heather continued, 'And don't tell me you have to work, because I know damn well you can get someone to cover for you if you need to.' She drew a slim book of tickets out of an oversized caramel leather purse I'd once admired when I'd seen it on the *Reporter*'s fashion spread, but whose price tag was way out of my range. 'Come on, you more than anyone ought to be helping out a charity that's raising money for research into heart disease, right?'

Eddie shrugged. 'OK, so how much is this going to set me back?'

'Well, the tickets are $500 each, and you'll be bringing your girlfriend, I take it?'

Girlfriend? I'd been working here for weeks, and this was the first I'd heard about Eddie having a girlfriend. My stomach did a sick little flip of disappointment, even as I wondered why the lucky lady had never so much as popped her head round the door in all that time.

'You take it correctly, sis.' Almost before I was aware of it, Eddie had wrapped an arm round my waist, pulling me to him. 'You'd love to come to this ball, wouldn't you, Summer?'

For a moment, both he and Heather stared at me intently, waiting for my answer. Not at all sure what was happening here, I stammered, 'Of course.'

'*She's* your girlfriend?' Heather sounded incredulous, eyeing me up and down. 'You've been telling me all about this fabulous girl of yours for so long now, I have to say I'd expected someone a little more – glamorous.'

'Says the woman who married her dry old stick of a boss,' Eddie retorted. 'How is Phillip, by the way?'

'He's fine. Waiting in the car outside. I have to drop

him at JFK to catch the early flight to London, so we don't have much time.'

Eddie took the hint, reaching in the breast pocket of his jacket and pulling out his cheque book. 'Who do I make it out to?'

'The Masquerade Ball,' Heather told him, watching as he filled in the cheque. Briefly, her glance settled on me once more. 'So, how did you two meet, exactly?'

I tried to catch Eddie's eye, but he was still busy writing. After his comment about Heather's husband, I had the feeling she wouldn't react too well if he admitted he was dating one of his staff, and I felt an almost insane urge to protect him from what I suspected was her whiplash tongue. Fortunately, the hooded top covered my T-shirt, which would have given my true status away at once.

The lie popped into my head from nowhere. 'Oh, I came in here one night with some friends to play pool and shoot the breeze. Eddie's eyes met mine over the bar counter and – well, we've been together ever since.' It all sounded so convincing, I almost believed it myself.

'Yeah, that's right,' Eddie agreed, adding a flourishing signature to his cheque, before tearing it out of the book and handing it to Heather. 'Summer's in advertising, works on the *Reporter*. A real hot prospect.'

Seemed two could bend the truth just as easily as one. Heather just sniffed, still clearly unimpressed. 'So, I'll see you at the Mallory. Seven for seven-thirty on Saturday.' She stashed the cheque in one of the inner pockets of her purse.

'Wouldn't miss it for the world, would we, honey?' Eddie pulled me close again, pressing a kiss to my lips. For a moment, I was almost too stunned to react, then I relaxed against him, revelling in the solid bulk of his body and his musky male smell, even as my mind fought to process the bizarre situation. I opened my mouth, feeling his tongue slip between my lips as the kiss deepened more than it might have had a right to. Then I broke away, flustered, hoping neither Eddie nor Heather could see the flush that had risen to my cheeks.

'Well, I'll see you Saturday, then.' The words "don't let me down" seemed to hang, unspoken, in the air between the three of us as Heather turned on her spike heel and strode out to her husband in the waiting car.

When she'd gone, Eddie smiled at me. 'Thanks for covering my ass, Summer.'

'No problem, but what exactly happened there? I kind of get the impression I've been invited to some swanky charity do, but ...' I didn't mention the kiss. I thought it safer not to.

'I'm sorry, I wish there was some kind of way I could have warned you, but I just didn't expect Heather to turn up out of the blue like that. I mean, you could probably tell we're not exactly close.'

'Close enough that if she tells you to jump, you jump.' I regretted the meanness of the words the second they'd left my mouth. Eddie simply acknowledged the barb.

'My dad died when I was 11, and my mom remarried about 18 months later. That's a difficult age to suddenly be landed with an older sister who you have absolutely nothing in common with. Someone who you know even then is way more driven and ambitious than you're ever going to be.'

'I'm sorry, I didn't mean to be rude.'

'But you do have a point. I try to keep Heather sweet because it's simplest all round. And I had promised ages ago that I'd go to this Masquerade Ball of hers; it just slipped my mind, what with having a barmaid up and quit on me and having to find a replacement, among other things.'

'So why did you tell her I was your girlfriend?'

'Ah, that.' He leant back against the bar, spreading his hands in an apologetic gesture. 'Well, Heather thinks I'm a loser for any number of reasons, chief of which is that I've never been able to hang on to a woman for any length of time. And the ones I do get involved with, she and my mom have never liked. They're always asking me when I'm going to meet a decent girl, not someone "fast and trashy", as my mom puts it. So – well, I kind of lied and told them I had. Luckily, I didn't go quite so far as to invent a name, or anything crazy like that. Truth is I've been single for the best part of a year now. So, rather than admit that when Heather confronted me just now, I – improvised. I hope you don't mind.'

Mind? If that kiss had been improvisation, he could do it again any time he liked. 'Not at all. But won't Heather be mad when she finds out she's been lied to?'

'Who says she's going to find out? Look, all I'm asking is for you to play the part of my girlfriend for the night. We'll turn up at the ball, and have a nice evening together. The next time she asks about you, I'll tell her that unfortunately it just didn't work out between the two of us.'

If I thought about the plan long enough, I was certain I'd find a flaw in it, but right now, I was still too busy digesting the information that I'd be going to the Masquerade Ball as Eddie Quinn's girlfriend.

When he said goodnight to me, I thought, just for a second, that he might kiss me again. But he didn't. Instead, like he did every night, he watched me walk away, till I rounded the corner of Hudson Street and we were lost to each other's view.

*   *   *

I lay awake for a long while that night, playing back the scene between Eddie, Heather, and me in my head. Eddie could have found some way of not going to the ball – hell, he could have simply made a contribution to whatever charity the event supported, but I suspected his sister would never let him off the hook that easily. Did she want the opportunity of judging his latest girlfriend, in the same way he claimed she'd judged all the rest and found them wanting? If so, what had I let myself in for – and, more importantly, where was I going to find an outfit suitable for a masquerade ball with only two days' notice?

Try as I might, though, I couldn't stop my thoughts drifting back to the moment when Eddie had planted that so unexpected kiss on my lips. I remembered the feel of his mouth, soft against my own, and the tickling of his beard against my cheeks. He only ever drank soft drinks while he was on duty behind the bar, and the kiss had carried the faint taste of cola, sweet and seductive. It might have been a performance for Heather's benefit, but I couldn't help thinking that he'd enjoyed kissing me more than he'd expected to; the way the pressure of his mouth had increased, and his hands had clutched at my back, pulling me on to his groin for the briefest instant, gave his enthusiasm away. If Heather hadn't been there, watching, what might have happened?

I pictured our clinch again. This time, we were alone in the darkened bar room, the jukebox switched off and silent, nothing to disturb our private moment. Our mouths locked together, tongues clashing as we kissed each other with a hunger that had been building since the moment I'd first walked through the door of the bar. He grabbed me by the hips, holding me tight to his crotch so I could feel the heft of his cock, straining to be free of his jeans. My passion stoked higher, I kissed him with sharp little pecks that were more like bites, sucking at the exposed, tanned skin of his neck above his T-shirt collar. He fumbled with my skirt, hitching it up almost to the tops of my thighs. With no pantyhose to impede his progress, it was easy for him to slip a finger under the lace of my panties and discover I was already wet. Too excited to hold back, he made to liberate his cock from the confines of his pants and press it to my waiting pussy.

Bringing myself back to the moment, I threw off the bedcovers, and reached for my vibrator, buried in the drawer of my nightstand. Powerful but whisper quiet, I'd bought it with one eye on not alerting the neighbours to my night-time self-pleasuring, though Tyler's antics with the blonde on the fire escape made me wonder how much the neighbours might actually care if they heard the buzzing of a sex toy coming through the walls.

I flicked on the switch, pressed the domed head of the vibrator to my sticky-wet pussy, and picked up the fantasy where I'd left it. Eddie had freed his erection from his jeans. It poked toward me insistently, juice beading on its tip. He rucked up my uniform T-shirt, and pulled my breasts free of my bra. His eagerness and overwhelming need for me excited me so much I couldn't stand it any longer. When I eased aside the crotch of my panties and pushed the head of his cock into my juicy hole, it slid in easily.

He was strong enough to support me with his weight while I wrapped my legs around his waist. He staggered back until I was half-sitting on the top of the bar counter, and started to thrust deeply into me. Every stroke slammed me back a little way on the polished wood, driving the breath from me. I clung on to him like a drowning woman, nails leaving pale half-moons in the flesh of his shoulders as we groaned and panted and shuddered together. His pubic bone ground against my clit, the short hairs around his balls rasping against the fabric of my panties, and he was nuzzling the hard points of my nipples, his face buried in my exposed cleavage.

In the fantasy, my inner muscles clamped down hard on Eddie's embedded length. In reality, it was the rigid silicone length of the vibrator that filled me as my orgasm bloomed deep inside me and I cried out Eddie's name, not caring if anyone heard me.

I felt sweat sticking my pyjama top to my back as I slowly came back to awareness of my surroundings. Switching off the vibrator, I let it drop to the floor.

So much heat generated from just a kiss – in my fantasy, at least. Playing Eddie's girlfriend was going to be fun, but I had to keep my feet on the ground. All he wanted was a one-night deal, convincing enough to fool his stepsister. Anything else had to remain purely in the realms of my imagination.

Chapter Four

FRIDAY MORNING FOUND ME ready to hunt on the rails of every thrift store in the Village, looking for a dress suitable for a masquerade ball. I couldn't afford to buy a new outfit, not when I knew I'd be unlikely to ever wear it again. Luckily, Heather hadn't specified a theme – if I'd needed to dress as a Southern Belle or Venetian lady, it would have meant an expensive trip to a costume hire shop. Men got it easy with these events; pretty much all they needed to do was throw on a tuxedo and a mask and they were good to go.

At least, living in an area with a high student population you were always guaranteed to find a few second-hand prom dresses for sale. In the third store I tried, I found just the thing. Strapless and made of wine-red satin, overlaid with a sheath of fine black lace, it came to just above my knees. I'd gained the impression Eddie was something of a leg man, and I intended to team the dress with sheer black thigh-high stockings and a pair of black lace pumps that lurked in the depths of my closet. When I tried it on, it was a little tight, but not uncomfortably so; as long as I didn't cut any extravagant moves on the dance floor, I figured the seams would hold. I couldn't help remembering the words Eddie said his mom used when talking about his previous girlfriends: "fast and trashy". I needed to give the impression of being sweet and sophisticated, however much it would have made Delia laugh to hear me described that way.

My mask came from a little store on West 4th Street that sold cheap party goods; plain gold, I could add sparkle to it by gluing on some glitter and a handful of little crystals. Hopefully, no one would realise I hadn't spent the $40 a similar mask would cost me from a high-end costume store.

Almost ridiculously pleased with my purchases, I treated myself to a Monte Cristo sandwich and a skinny latte in a little café, taking the opportunity to sit and watch the world go by. No matter how long I lived in Greenwich Village, I'd thought I'd never get tired of the passing parade: fashionistas chattering on their cell phones as they took their little dogs for a walk, the animal so small they could easily fit it in their oversized purse; musicians clutching guitar cases as they headed to rehearsals, or the gig they were sure would help them land that elusive record deal; students, laughing and arguing and carrying themselves with all the confidence of someone who thinks the world can one day belong to them.

Every time I considered how lucky I was to have an affordable apartment in such a desirable area, I had to pinch myself. The landlord was an old friend of my grandmother's, and when I'd been looking for somewhere to live in my college days, she used her not inconsiderable charm on him to persuade him to let the place out to me at well below the market rate. Recently, though, he seemed to have taken notice of how much real estate had become worth around here, and was talking about selling up, and moving to some retirement complex in Florida. A new landlord would set about fixing the plumbing and giving the building the renovation it so badly needed, pushing the rent way beyond my means when the work was finished. But I'd worry about that when it happened. For now, my focus remained on making sure I didn't let Eddie down at the ball.

By the time Saturday evening came round, I was a mess of nerves. Eddie had told me he'd call round to collect me at around 6.45, so we could take a cab up to Central Park West and the Mallory Hotel together. I hadn't been able to share the fact we were going to the Masquerade Ball with anyone. I'd rung Delia for a girly conversation, only for her to tell me she was at her mom's home for a family celebration, and she'd talk to me when she got back, and somehow it didn't seem fair to mention it to Penny, who was working the Friday night shift alongside me. She'd been an employee of Eddie's for far longer than me; by rights, she ought to be the one accompanying him to the ball. Though maybe her boyfriend, who was one of the leading lights of the NYU track team, might have something to say if she did.

For once, the water heater was behaving itself, and I'd taken a long, hot bath, exfoliating from head to toe before applying body lotion that left a hint of glitter on my skin. I'd thought about pouring a glass of wine to drink in the tub, to give me a little Dutch courage, then decided against it. In my new dress and with darker, smokier eye make-up than I usually wore – even though I knew my eyes would be hidden behind the mask all evening, I still wanted to create an impact – I felt like a different person. Someone daring; someone who gave in to their impulses, rather than standing on the sidelines, watching life go on all around them.

I was admiring my new look in the mirror, examining my reflection from all angles, when the door buzzer rang. Almost tripping over my heels in my haste to answer it, I pressed the button and said, 'Yes?'

'Hey, Summer, it's Eddie.'

'Come on up. I'm on the third floor.' I heard the snick as I pushed the door release, and turned my attention to putting my phone and wallet into my evening bag. Eddie must have taken the stairs two at a time, because it seemed like only moments before he was knocking at my apartment door. 'Be right with you,' I called, slicking more gloss over already shiny lips.

When I opened the door, we both stared at each other. Apart from the afternoon I'd walked into his bar and wangled the job, he'd never seen me in anything other than his staff uniform, and as far as I was concerned, he lived in T-shirt and jeans. So for a moment, we were strangers meeting for the first time.

Delia and I had had a long, Cosmopolitan-fuelled conversation one night, debating whether a guy looked hotter in smart or casual clothes. At the time, I'd asserted that nothing could be sexier than the all-time classic combination of blue jeans and a plain white T-shirt, and until now I'd continued to believe that. Looking at Eddie in his form-fitting black tuxedo was causing me to revise that opinion rapidly. He hadn't gone so far as to get a haircut or shave his beard as a concession to the occasion, but that just added to his charm, at least as far as I was concerned. I wasn't sure his stepsister would see it in quite the same way.

As for Eddie, his eyes were wide as he gazed at me, and he seemed almost too surprised to speak. At last, he said, 'Wow. Summer – you look incredible.'

'So you think Heather will approve?' I asked.

'I approve, and that's all that matters.' He grinned. 'Come on, let's go get a cab.'

I grabbed my coat, locked the door behind me, and we began to make our way down the dark, gloomy staircase,

Eddie moderating his pace so I could keep up with him in my teetering heels. As we emerged on to the sidewalk, Kenny, who owned the comic book store that occupied the basement floor of the building, was climbing the black-painted iron steps, having just shut the store for the evening.

Just as Eddie had done, he took a moment to take in my extravagant appearance. 'Hi, Summer, off somewhere nice?'

'The Masquerade Ball at the Mallory,' I told him. 'This is Eddie, my boss, by the way.'

'Oh, so you're the famous Eddie.' Kenny took Eddie's hand, pumping it up and down in an enthusiastic handshake. 'Summer's told me how great you are to work for. Though you know if it doesn't work out –' he turned to me, expression sincere '– I can always use an extra pair of hands in the Comic Cavern.'

'That's a kind offer, Kenny, but me and comic books, we don't really mix. Like Spiderman and kryptonite, you know.'

'I think you mean Superman,' Eddie corrected me.'

'See what I mean? Thanks, anyway.' At that moment, a yellow cab rounded the corner, and Eddie stepped into the road to flag it down.

'Well, enjoy, both of you,' Kenny said, waving us off as we climbed into the cab and fastened our seatbelts.

Once Eddie had given the driver our destination, he fixed me with a quizzical look. 'The famous Eddie? What's that all about?'

'Oh, Kenny and I are always bumping into each other outside the shop, and we chat sometimes. It's true, I told him you're a great boss to work for, but that's because you are.'

He said nothing, but a little smile tugged at the corners

of his mouth, as though he was quietly appreciating the compliment. We travelled in silence for half-a-dozen blocks, hitting every green light as we turned on to Eighth Avenue, then a sudden thought seemed to strike Eddie. 'You have got your mask, haven't you?'

I nodded, pulling it out of my bag and holding it to my eyes. In return, Eddie fished a small black domino mask from his tux pocket. 'I'm gonna feel kind of foolish wearing this thing all night,' he grumbled. 'I mean, it's bad enough that I've had to get into the monkey suit ...'

If only you knew how gorgeous you look, I wanted to tell him, but we were both distracted by the cabbie stabbing the horn with the heel of his hand and yelling a bunch of Russian-sounding curse words at the cyclist who'd just cut him up at the lights.

Minutes later, the cab pulled up on Central Park West, in front of the impressive Art Deco façade of the Mallory Hotel. Eddie glanced at the meter, opened his wallet, and handed over a fistful of bills to the driver, telling him to keep the change.

'Let me know what I owe you,' I said.

He shook his head. 'This is on me. I assume you've had to go out and buy that outfit specially for tonight. It doesn't seem fair to ask you to contribute to the cab fare as well.'

The liveried doorman nodded and wished us a polite good evening as he held open the entrance door for us. I had to keep pinching myself as we walked into the Mallory's lobby, with its marble floor and ornate crystal chandeliers hanging from the high ceiling. None of this felt real; I had to be dreaming. But if I was, I didn't want to wake up, not when Eddie was giving me the smile that never failed to turn me inside-out, and reaching to slip his mask over his head.

'OK, here goes,' he said.

I mimicked his action, fixing my mask in place. We followed a stream of other guests, most of the men in simple dinner suits but the women wearing much more lavish outfits than my own, into the hotel ballroom. A table plan stood by the door, and Eddie gave it a cursory check.

'Table 13. Lucky for some,' he commented.

'Lucky?' I queried.

'Yeah, Heather and Phillip look to be sitting on the other side of the room to us.'

A waiter went by, carrying a tray laden with glasses of champagne. Eddie snagged a couple as he passed, handed one to me, and clinked his glass against mine, proposing a toast. 'Here's to being whatever – and whoever – we want to be tonight.'

'I'll drink to that,' I replied, a pulse beating hard between my legs as my body flooded with heat. In this exotic atmosphere, identity suddenly became very fluid. Given the masks that covered everyone's faces, no one had any idea whether they were standing next to a top executive who earned a seven-figure salary, or a lowly sales clerk. It felt like anything could happen tonight.

I took a good look round the room, trying to print as many of the details as I could on my memory so I could share them with Delia the next time I saw her. Of course, what I really wanted to tell her was not that a seven-piece band occupied a raised dais, playing cover versions of songs by Lady Gaga and Britney Spears, or that guests were able to help themselves to shots from a vodka luge, its ice sculpted in the form of the Statue of Liberty. No, I was more concerned with watching Eddie as he ran a hand through his hair, keeping a wary eye out for the possible approach of Heather. Despite his complaints, he looked comfortable in his tuxedo; I supposed the outfit appealed to the lurking belief every guy has that, in the right circumstances, he'd make the perfect secret agent.

The evening's MC, a local TV newsreader whose voice was instantly recognisable even if his face was partially disguised, made an announcement asking us to take our places at the dinner table. Eddie and I found ourselves sitting with a party from one of the big law firms on Lexington Avenue. Luckily for us, they didn't want to talk shop all night. Instead, they seemed more interested in learning from Eddie what it took to run a bar. He regaled them with stories of some of the strangest customers he'd had to deal with over the years, from the guy who bought a round for everyone in the bar to celebrate the fact his divorce was final to the couple who'd started off with a spot of dirty dancing to the jukebox and had to be stopped from outright fucking on the pool table. Occasionally, he'd brush my palm with his fingers, or turn and fix me with a gaze from behind his mask, keeping up the illusion that we really were a long-time couple. Whenever he did, a shivery heat ran through me, and I found it hard to concentrate on whatever was being said.

The food was delicious – a delicate smoked fish mousse to start, followed by Cornish game hens served with wild rice and roasted vegetables, and strawberry cake with white chocolate ice cream for dessert – and the wine was a cut above anything Eddie sold in the bar. During the meal, entertainers moved between the tables: caricaturists drew lightning-quick sketches of the guests, and magicians performed tricks involving cards and coins, working their sleight of hand to a rapturous reception. Even though Eddie and Heather appeared not to be particularly close, which only served to prejudice me against her, I couldn't help but admire the effort she and her colleagues on the charity committee had put into organising the event.

As waiters appeared to remove the dessert plates and serve coffee to those who wanted it, Eddie excused himself to go to the restroom. Almost before I was aware of it, a woman took his seat. Like the rest of the entertainers, she wasn't masked. She wore a blue chiffon top with voluminous sleeves, and silver half-moons dangled from her earlobes. I pegged her as a fortune teller before she even opened her mouth.

'You have an amazingly vivid aura, honey,' she told me in the sing-song tones of a Louisiana native. New Orleans, I guessed, where they took precognitive powers pretty seriously. Certainly more seriously than I did. 'I saw it clear across the room. Bright pink, the colour of creativity, sensuality, and new relationships. May I have your hand?'

I wanted to suggest she use her mind-reading tricks on someone else on our table, uncomfortable with her attention for no reason I could fathom, but that would have been rude. So I let her take my fingers in a loose grip, and waited for her to start pointing out what the lines on my palm meant.

Instead, she closed her eyes tight, her face a mask of concentration. 'There's been a big upheaval in your life very recently,' she said at length. 'I see new surroundings, somewhere with music playing, and old wooden furniture. Does the name O'Malley mean anything to you?'

With a chill, I thought of Sergeant O'Malley's portrait, hanging above the bar at Eddie's. 'Actually, it does.'

'It's not what you're used to, but it makes you happy.' Opening her eyes, she smiled at me. 'And so does he.' He? Could she be talking about Eddie? 'But trouble is coming, and you need to ignore those who wish to make mischief. Listen to your heart.'

Now that sounded like a line from one of the corny pop songs the band had been playing earlier; vague and insubstantial where her previous pronouncements had been strangely accurate. Before she could add anything that might make her statement clearer, Eddie reappeared, standing at the side of his occupied chair and looking from the interloper to me with a quizzical expression. The fortune teller broke her grip on my arm, and stood. 'I'll leave that for you to think on.' With that, she moved on to the neighbouring table, no doubt looking for another dinner guest with an enticing aura.

'What was going on there?' Eddie asked, plopping himself down on the chair by my side.

'I got my future told.' I took a sip of coffee, letting its rich taste ground me back in the real world. 'She said a tall, dark man would appear in my life – and here you are. So I can't fault her for accuracy.'

On the little stage, the band struck up again, launching into the opening bars of a 70s disco classic. Drawn by the music, people rose from their tables and headed for the dance floor. 'Wanna dance?' Eddie extended a hand. When I hesitated, he continued, 'Come on, Summer. I'm sure Heather's keeping an eye out for me, and I want her to see us having a good time. She's gonna be reporting back to Mom the first chance she gets.'

'OK, then let's give her something to talk about,' I said, and followed him on to the dance floor.

To my surprise, he moved well; not one of these flashy dancers who's determined to be noticed by everyone around them, but someone comfortable with the beat and his own body. I've heard it said how a man dances is meant to be an indication of what he'll be like in bed, but

I don't hold much store by that. Todd was never much of a dancer, but in the short time we were together he proved he knew what to do between the sheets well enough.

'You know, I never figured you for someone who could dance,' I admitted, as the music slowed, changing to a number designed to encourage couples to hold each other close.

'Used to do a bit of boxing when I was a kid,' Eddie replied, wrapping a brawny arm around me. Even in my heels, my head only came up to the point of his chin. 'You need to be light on your feet when you're moving round the ring.'

'You don't fight any more?' I asked.

'Nah. I keep a punchbag in my basement for when I need to let off a bit of steam.' He grinned. 'It gets you into less trouble than punching a customer.'

As we swayed together, Eddie's body pressed tightly against mine, I saw Heather standing by the edge of the dance floor, in conversation with a man in a white tuxedo. She'd given a small speech of welcome once we'd all been seated for dinner, thanking us for attending and giving a brief outline of how our donations would be used to provide life-saving equipment for those suffering a rare form of degenerative heart disease. Remembering her comments to Eddie in the bar, I'd wondered as she'd been talking whether this disease was what had killed his father, but somehow it didn't seem the right time to ask.

Now I looked at her again, ash-blonde hair styled in a sleek up-do, and wearing a sheath dress of ice-blue and silver tones that flattered her cool colouring. Her face was hidden behind a silver half mask that curved up over her left eye in the shape of a crescent moon, but from the movement of her head it was clear she was watching Eddie and me. I wondered whether she bought the act that we'd been together for a while – the lawyers on our table certainly seemed to think that, though they'd never met us before tonight.

And as Eddie held me a little closer and I rested my head on the wide expanse of his shoulder, I wondered just how much of an act this was. We might be able to fake some aspects of our so-called relationship, but the steady pressure of his rising cock against my belly was all too real. Grinding against me as we danced was clearly turning him on. The thought of what that cock might look like, freed from his formal attire and standing proud, made my pussy clench with desire.

Maybe I should have pulled away, made some excuse to go back to our table in an attempt to defuse what had the potential to become a pretty awkward situation. After all, we were only pretending to want each other so badly – weren't we?

Eddie didn't seem in the least embarrassed by his growing erection. His hand trailed down from its relatively chaste position in the small of my back, coming to rest on my ass cheek. His palm felt hot through the satin and lace of my clothing, though that could just have been down to my feverish imagination magnifying every sensation. I wanted him to stroke that cheek, squeeze it, maybe even give it a hard slap or two to stimulate the little, hidden part of me that got off on a man displaying his dominant streak. Then I shook my head. I shouldn't be having fantasies like this; not here, not now.

Except Eddie must have been having similar fantasies too. Just for a moment, his hand smoothed over my ass in possessive fashion. His caress set me tingling, and when I looked up, his lips curved in a secretive smile and he bent to kiss me, angling his head so our masks wouldn't become tangled together. The touch of his warm, soft lips on mine was the most delightful shock, more unexpected in its way than when he'd kissed me in the bar to make a point to Heather. But this time it didn't seem like he was kissing me for anyone's benefit other than his own, and I melted into his embrace, letting his tongue push between my lips to take ownership of my mouth. We'd stopped moving, oblivious to the couples still dancing around us, both of Eddie's hands on my ass now and my body a breathless, needy mess as his teeth nipped gently at my lower lip.

When we finally broke apart, he sounded almost apologetic. 'Summer, I didn't mean to – That is, I saw Heather keeping an eye on us and –'

So as far as he was concerned, it had all been part of the act, and I'd been a fool to react to his kiss as strongly as I did. But that didn't explain why his cock was harder than ever, nudging urgently at me as if seeking to bore its way through my dress, or why his eyes glittered with lust behind his mask.

About to turn and leave the dance floor so I could gather my thoughts and decide whether going home now might be the most sensible option, his next words stilled me in my tracks. 'But once I started kissing you, I didn't think I'd ever be able to stop. Summer, I don't know what I thought might happen between us tonight, but all I know is I want you more than I've wanted anyone for a hell of a long time.' He took my hand, his thumb gently stroking my palm. His voice was low, deliciously insinuating a path all the way down to my tense, aching pussy. 'You can say no and we can call an end to this right now, or I can go to the front desk and see whether they have a room available for the night.'

Maybe I'd had the odd fantasy where Eddie and I shared a taxi home at the end of the night, and we'd found ourselves having coffee – and more – at my place, but I'd never seriously dreamt I might find myself being asked so blatantly whether I wanted to sneak away in the middle of the revelry to sleep with him. "No" had no place in my vocabulary at this moment; this might be the only chance I got to spend the night in Eddie Quinn's arms, and I had no intention of turning him down. There might be repercussions, but I was a big girl; I'd deal with them when they arose. Now all I could do was nod and say, 'Let's do it.'

He led me off the dance floor and out of the ballroom. My heels clicked on the lobby's marble tiles as I scurried to keep up with him. It seemed once Eddie had a plan of action in his mind, he was determined to carry it out as soon as possible; he'd claimed he wasn't as single-minded as his stepsister, but looking at him now, he had his moments.

Following a brief conversation with the perky brunette on the front desk, while I waited on a low and extremely comfortable leather chesterfield, Eddie turned to me with a grin. He clutched a key card in his hand. 'We're in luck. They must keep a few rooms back for ball guests who overdo it and aren't in any state to get home. We're in Room 914.'

Holding out a hand, he helped me up from the sofa. My heart thudded in my chest as we waited for the elevator, so loud I was sure Eddie could hear it; I was giddy with anticipation. The doors opened; there were no other passengers, and Eddie pushed me up against the glass wall of the elevator and picked up where we'd left off on the dance floor. His mouth devoured mine with hot, greedy kisses, and his hands skimmed my breasts, my nipples all too hard and obvious even the layers of clothing I now desperately wanted to be rid of.

The elevator climbed swiftly, but I barely noticed the floors passing, lost in the touch and taste of Eddie. His leg nudged its way insistently between my thighs, my dress hiking up in the process, till the ridge of his kneecap rubbed against my panty-covered mound, the dull friction sparking fresh prickles of sensation throughout my body. My fantasies of what it would be like to be kissed by him, to have him take charge in this way, had been good, but they couldn't match the reality.

When the elevator doors opened on the ninth floor, it didn't register with either of us that we'd arrived at our destination. Only as they began to slide shut again did Eddie realise where we were, jabbing at the button to stop them closing fully. We dashed out on to the silent, thickly carpeted hallway, looking for a sign to point us in the direction of Room 914.

'This way,' Eddie said, pointing to the left. He found our room four doors along, and pushed the key into the slot. The light turned green, the lock buzzed and clicked, and we were inside. I took only the most cursory look at our surroundings, gathering an impression of heavy brown drapes at the window, muted wall coverings, and a bed heaped high with pillows. Eddie still claimed my full attention, peeling out of his jacket, and tugging at his bow tie, so the ends dangled loose against his shirt front. He popped open his top shirt button, then the one below it. Lust bubbled through me as the flat, lightly furred plane of his chest came into view.

He kicked off his shoes, and lay back on the bed.

'Strip for me, Summer,' he urged. Propped against the pillows, he looked like he was settling in to enjoy the show.

'Don't you want me to pull the drapes first?' I asked. Our room was on the side of the hotel, with a view out to the buildings across the way, and I was conscious that someone might look out of one of the windows and see what we were doing.

'Leave them,' he ordered. 'Maybe we'll give someone a thrill. I mean, as long as we keep our masks on, who'll know who we are?'

My mind flashed back to the morning I'd watched Tyler and his blonde girlfriend fucking on the fire escape, remembering how excited I'd got on that occasion. So this was how Eddie wanted to play it, was it? Well, I had no intention of disappointing him. Reaching behind me, I unzipped my dress, sighing as I was freed from its constricting hold. I let it slither to the floor in a rustle of lace, then took a couple of paces closer to the bed, unclipping my bra as I did. Eddie's eyes, dark wells of desire, never left me as I removed the garment, holding the cups tight to my chest with one hand while I slipped the straps off my shoulders with the other, promising everything but revealing nothing. Shirtless now, he stroked himself through his trousers as he watched me, and I yearned for him to loose his cock so I could see it in all its glory.

At last, I let my bra drop, giving Eddie a brief, teasing glimpse of my breasts before clamping my palms over them once more.

'Show me,' he urged. 'Show me everything.'

The raw need in his voice almost had me creaming my panties. Beneath his strong, masculine assurance lurked a vulnerable core; only when a man trusted you enough would he open up and let you see that side of him, and already Eddie seemed prepared to offer me a glimpse into his secret self. How long would it be before –? I brought myself up short. No point in thinking about what might happen in the future. This was all about tonight.

'OK, but you've got to show me something too. Seems only fair, don't you think?'

He conceded the point with a nod, and his hands flew to unzip his fly. Until now, I'd never thought a man could shimmy out of his pants in any kind of elegant fashion while lying on the bed, but Eddie managed it, kicking the garment off first one leg, than the next. His plain white shorts stretched tight across his groin, as if fighting to contain the delights within, a damp spot visible on the front bearing witness to his excitement.

He looked to me, expecting me to reciprocate by taking off something else, but I shook my head. 'Socks and underwear. Really not a look that turns a girl on.'

'So which of them do you want me to lose?' He grinned.

I don't care, I wanted to tell him. I just want you bare for me. Bare and hard. It seemed he didn't need an answer to the question, though, because he was already bringing his legs up toward his ass, folding himself in half so he could peel off his socks.

'Now you.'

This time, I didn't stall. I made to roll down one of my stockings, but Eddie stopped me. 'No, keep those on,' he ordered. 'And the heels. I love the way they look.'

That meant I had to take off my panties. Shy of revealing myself completely to Eddie, even though he'd already given every sign of liking what he saw, I wriggled out of the wet wisp of fabric as demurely as I could.

He said nothing, but the lust in his gaze told me everything I needed to know. I'd never felt so thoroughly desired as I stood there, waiting for him to respond in kind. Without any of the modesty I'd shown, he rose from the bed and shucked off his underwear. The expression on my face as I stared at his cock, revealed in its full majesty, must have rivalled his in its unashamed need, for he chuckled.

'I'm sorry, I –' I began, even though I didn't quite know what I was apologising for.

'Hey, come here, Summer...' Crossing the short stretch of carpet that separated us in a couple of strides, he pulled me into an embrace just as close as the one we'd shared on the dance floor, only now the hot, jutting length of him pressed directly into my bare belly. His lips crushed mine in a searching kiss; his hands moulded themselves to my ass and his tongue plundered my mouth. In reply, I pushed my hand down between our bodies and gripped his shaft, unable to keep myself from stroking that gorgeous tool.

He broke the kiss and stepped back, bending to pick up his smart pants from the floor, and I thought for one horrible moment I'd crossed some unstated line and he was calling a halt to proceedings. Instead, he fumbled his wallet out of the back pocket, rifling through it till he found a condom.

'You can always tell me if you don't want this,' he said, fixing me with a look that told me how important it was I answered him honestly.

On fire for him, I replied, 'Oh, I want this.' And damn the consequences.

'That's all I needed to know.' He tore open the foil, skinning on the condom while I ran my fingers over the wet terrain of my pussy. Downstairs, the ball would still be in full swing, but at this moment, the world came down to just the two of us.

We fell on each other again, lips locked together. Eddie steered me backwards, until I butted up against the window. Apart from a thick plaster-covered sill about six inches high, it ran the full height of the room. Giving all control over to him, I let Eddie guide me up onto that sill, and spin me round so I faced out into the night. My stomach lurched; anyone looking out from one of the buildings across the way, or glancing up from the street below could not fail to see me, my naked body pressed against the glass. Yet with the golden mask disguising my features, I was truly anonymous; some mystery woman about to get the fucking of her life from an equally naked, equally masked lover.

One of Eddie's hands came round in front of me, gripping my tits and pinching the nipples till I gasped with the sweet, tormenting pain. His other hand he used to guide his cock to my pussy opening. 'Are you ready?' he asked.

'God, yes.' I felt him slide just the tip of his dick inside me, teasing me with a taste of what he had to offer until I moaned and thrust my ass back at his groin, urgent to have more of him filling me up.

When he obliged, I thought I'd never known until this moment how good it could be to have a man's cock lodged in the slick depths of my cunt, fitting so well it could have been designed just for me. Despite that, we struggled to find a rhythm at first, our blind need for each other, and our unfamiliarity with the other's body, making our movements awkward. Even though Eddie had already brought me closer to his own height by placing me on the window sill, I found it was easier if I stood on tiptoe, the position allowing him to thrust deeper.

Nine floors below us, out on the street, I could see cars passing, headlights cutting a path through the darkness while I was having the wild, spontaneous sex I'd been dreaming of ever since the morning I'd watched that dirty little exhibition on the fire escape.

Eddie's mouth nuzzled at the side of my neck, and his

hand made a swift descent of my body, coming to rest between my parted thighs.

'Do it,' I begged him. 'Make me come.'

His thrusts increased in their ferocity, pushing me harder against the glass, making me glad the window pane was triple-glazed, more than thick enough to withstand the pressure. All the while, his finger skated over my clit, driving me towards an orgasm that threatened to break me in two. When I came, I threw my head back and yelled out my pleasure, loud enough to wake anyone who might be sleeping in the neighbouring rooms. Eddie followed moments behind, clinging tight to me as he emptied everything he had into the condom.

When we pulled apart, he swept me up in his arms and carried me over to the bed, laying me down gently. I removed my mask, and the heels and stockings, while Eddie tossed the condom in the trash and put his own mask on the nightstand.

'You'll stay the night, won't you?' he said, settling in behind me so our bodies spooned together, his groin pressed against the curve of my ass.

'Do you think it's a good idea?' I asked, even though all I wanted to do was fall asleep in his arms, secure and protected.

'Would I be asking if I didn't? Besides, it might look a bit odd if you walked out on me now.' Eddie dropped a kiss on my shoulder. 'Thanks for everything, Summer. For putting on such a great show downstairs, and for –' He paused. 'I mean, when I asked you to be my partner tonight I'd didn't think we'd actually end up going as far as we did, but …'

I rolled over to face him. Somehow, it felt strange to be looking right into his face, no longer obscured by the domino mask. 'You don't regret it, do you?' My tone was more anxious than I liked the sound of. 'I mean, I don't want things to be awkward between us next time I come into work.'

He shook his head. 'I have no regrets, I promise you. It was incredible. *You* were incredible. You know, for a fake girlfriend, Summer, you're better than the real thing.'

'Thanks, Eddie – I think.'

When he gave me a drowsy grin, I experienced again the same melting sensation I had when I'd first met him in the bar, the same flood of warmth and excitement. He murmured something that sounded an awful lot like, 'I really think I'm falling in love with you,' but when I asked him to repeat what he'd just said, his only response was a soft snore.

Still trying to decipher what I'd just heard, I closed my eyes. Sleep came more quickly than I'd expected, and when it did, my dreams were all of Eddie.

Chapter Five

WHEN I WOKE, EDDIE lay asleep beside me, curled on his right side, his broad back facing me. I couldn't be entirely sure, but in the half-light it looked as though I'd left scratch marks on his skin, carried away in the heat of passion.

Just thinking about what we'd done last night made my pussy flutter, already eager for more despite the faint soreness between my thighs. The prospect was tempting, but as I watched Eddie slumber so peacefully, I knew I had to leave. The moment I stopped thinking of this as a one time only deal, started believing what I thought I'd heard Eddie say in the moments before he'd drifted off to sleep, I risked opening myself up to all kinds of hurt and heartache. I'd played the part he'd asked of me, and now it was time to quit the stage.

A glance at my watch let me know it was gone 7 a.m. The bakery on West 4th would be open by now; I could stop in on my way home and pick up a Danish for breakfast. Careful not to wake Eddie, I shrugged on my bra, then zipped myself into the prom dress. My panties I couldn't locate anywhere, and I wasn't in the mood to go hunting for them. Eddie could keep them as a souvenir, if he found them tangled among his own clothing.

Even though I knew it was the right thing to do, it somehow felt wrong to leave without saying goodbye. A notepad, each page monogrammed with the Mallory's logo, stood on the nightstand. I reached for the pen by its side, and quickly wrote "Thanks so much for last night. See you at work", signing the note with my initial and a big, scrawled kiss. Then I quietly let myself out of the room. Eddie didn't appear to have stirred.

The elevator arrived almost as soon as I pressed the button, and I stepped inside. In the seconds before the door closed, I thought I heard someone call my name, but put it down to guilty thoughts about running out on Eddie. I tried not to catch a glimpse of my reflection in its mirrored walls, or think back to how my gorgeous boss had pressed me against those walls on our way up, his big hands all over my body as we'd kissed.

I was halfway across the lobby, congratulating myself on having made a successful escape, when I heard a voice call my name. Looking round, I saw Heather sitting on the chesterfield, smiling at me. Unlike me, she'd brought a change of clothes, looking neat and prim in a long-sleeved floral dress; no walk of shame for her this morning.

I couldn't pretend not to have recognised her, so I walked over. 'Hi, Heather, thanks for putting on such a great event. We had a fantastic time last night.'

'Eddie not with you?' She rose from her seat, looking at me in a way that made me uncomfortable, though I couldn't have said quite why.

'Oh, he likes to sleep in. I'm just popping out for some breakfast.' It wasn't entirely a lie. 'What about you?'

'I'm waiting for Phillip to come down. I've just got a couple of things to sort out with the hotel manager, then we're off to have our monthly brunch with Phillip's mother in East Hampton.' Despite the breeziness of her tone, something suggested she found these get-togethers a chore. 'But I'm so pleased you enjoyed yourself. You know, what I love about events like this is the chance to catch up with people you haven't seen in ages. In fact, would you believe I was talking to someone who knows you over dinner?'

I didn't have a clue who she was talking about, and she must have seen that on my face. 'Really?'

'Yes, an old friend of mine, Rebecca Haynes.' She waited for the impact of the name to sink in, clearly relishing the fact she had me on the back foot. 'She and I go way back. We were in business school together. She was really intrigued when I mentioned my stepbrother was dating one of her staff.'

God, Eddie had told Heather I sold ads on the *Reporter*, hadn't he? My stomach gave a sick lurch.

'You know, Summer, it's the damnedest thing. When I mentioned your name Heather said you hadn't actually worked at the *Reporter* for over a month now. In fact, she told me that she had to let you go. Poor timekeeping, persistent failure to meet targets, bad attitude, Crazy Color in your hair – any of that sounding familiar?'

OK, so I hadn't exactly been the model employee, but Rebecca had clearly oversold my faults in a major way. I started to protest, but Heather cut me off. 'So, does Eddie know you don't actually work at the *Reporter* any more, or are you spinning him a line so he doesn't realise what a failure you are? And could you be lying to him about anything else? I mean, Rebecca told me that you and some little friend of yours were always bragging about the rich, flashy guys you met in bars. You're not maybe still meeting those guys behind my stepbrother's back, by any chance?'

'Oh, that's total bull –' I began, but a stocky, silver-haired man, looking rather ill at ease in a raspberry polo shirt and khaki chinos, had come hurrying over.

'Is this girl bothering you, darling?' he asked, casting

an anxious glance from Heather to me.

'No, Phillip, it's fine,' Heather assured him. 'Eddie's little tramp of a girlfriend was just leaving, weren't you, Summer?'

My hackles were up and I bristled with anger, but I knew better than to make any kind of scene, not when the girl at the front desk was looking our way, no doubt wondering whether she ought to be calling security. So I turned and headed for the door, holding my head as high as I could, not wanting Heather to see how her words had wounded me.

Central Park West seemed eerily deserted as I walked down to the 72nd Street subway station; too early for the tourists to be out, too late for the night birds and last straggling clubbers. At least no one was around to see me, coat pulled tight over my beautiful, too-tight dress, trying to blink away the tears that stung my eyes.

Somehow, I just knew that as soon as Heather had the chance, she'd confront Eddie, letting him know I was a liar, a loser, and most likely a slut too, even though I hadn't dated anyone since Todd, and before him – well, I couldn't even remember. What had Rebecca said, that Delia and I had "bragged" about the guys we picked up? I didn't remember any bragging; usually just me consoling Delia when her latest conquest turned out to be married, or some other shade of sleazebag. But the information would have reached Rebecca via a sneaky little chain of Chinese whispers that started and ended with Mary Lou, who'd never been able to resist making me look bad. Or Delia, for that matter. A sudden guilty pang shot through me about the way my best friend was being dragged into a situation that really shouldn't involve her; a situation that, when you looked at it rationally, boiled down to some pointless little family squabble.

Not that I could be mad at Eddie for what he'd said to Heather. He'd only been trying to protect me when he claimed I was in ad sales, wanting to spare both of us from whatever tongue-lashing she'd choose to dish out on learning he was dating one of his staff. Yet I'd still ended up taking a torrent of unfounded accusation from her, based on the word of my former boss, who loathed me as much as I loathed her, and with no opportunity to fight back. Although what would that have achieved? Heather had made her mind up about me the night she'd first seen me in the bar, and even if I managed to end world famine and discover a cure for cancer, it wouldn't change her opinion one whit.

At the ticket booth, I tried not to catch the eye of the woman behind the toughened glass as I handed over the money for my fare. I supposed she saw distressed-looking passengers all the time, but I knew if I received a look from anyone that was even vaguely sympathetic, I would break down and cry.

My footsteps echoed in the vast, empty expanse of the station as I descended the steps to the platform. On a weekday, any number of commuters would have been hurrying past me, jostling for space, but now I pretty much had the length of the platform to myself. The downtown train arrived, and I slumped into the seat nearest to the door, burying my head in my hands.

I couldn't go back to working at Eddie's, not after this. I'd been prepared to accept that we could only enjoy one glorious night of sex together, just as long as we could return to the relaxed, comfortable working relationship we'd had before. Everything we'd said to each other before we'd fallen asleep had led me to believe that would be the case. But whatever bombshell Heather chose to drop would make it impossible. He'd never be able to look at me the same way, not if she managed to convince him I really was the kind of girl who went out and picked up men for the hell of it, and who might choose to keep on doing so even while she was in a relationship.

When I emerged from the subway at West 4th, I checked my phone through force of habit, as I always did whenever I'd been underground a while. No one had rung. On impulse, I called up Delia's number, even though I knew she'd more than likely still be asleep in her old bedroom at her mom's house. When her recorded voice kicked in, asking whoever was calling to leave a message, I blurted, 'Hey, Delia, it's Summer. Give me a ring as soon as you get this, would you? I really need to talk to you.'

Shoving the phone back in my purse, I headed for the baker's, needing the comfort of a warm, sticky pastry more than ever. Unable to choose between the oven-fresh cinnamon roll and the raspberry Danish, I bought both. When I got home, I'd brew a pot of coffee and gorge myself on sweet things. Then I'd sit and consider my future. Kenny had told me there was a job at the Comic Cavern if I ever wanted it. Maybe spending my day surrounded by nerds wouldn't be all bad; some of them might even be cute, though I doubted any of them would be willing to put up with my inability to tell my *Star Wars* from my *Star Trek*.

I took a different way home for once, so I didn't have to walk past Eddie's. Even though he wouldn't be there, just the sight of the bar would stir up feelings I was trying hard to keep buried.

The climb up to my apartment seemed to take twice as long as usual. I hadn't bothered to put on my stockings when I'd dressed, and my shoes were rubbing sore spots on the backs of my heels. As soon as I was through the door, I got changed, pulling on a comfortable robe. When I'd had breakfast, I intended to take a long bath, easing the slight soreness between my legs and washing the last traces of Eddie from my skin. In other circumstances, I would have wanted to keep any reminder of him, and the way he'd made me feel as his cock ploughed into my snug depths, for as long as possible. But it was all over now. Best to let the memories go.

I'd just torn a piece from the cinnamon roll and popped it into my mouth when my cell phone rang. Swallowing it down, wiping my fingers so as not to cover the phone in sticky frosting, I answered with a brisk, 'Hey, Delia, thanks for ringing me back ...'

'This isn't Delia.' Eddie's voice interrupted. If I'd bothered to look at the display, I'd have known that wasn't the case. Hell, if I'd seen it was Eddie calling I'd have let it ring unanswered. I didn't want to speak to him, but I didn't have the heart to put the phone down on him.

'Hi Eddie. How are you?'

'Fine. Hoping I might get invited up.'

'Why? Where are you?' I'd assumed he was calling from the Mallory, but the hooting of a car horn on the other end of the phone told me that wasn't the case. A hooting that, I realised, sounded very like the one I could hear through the open window of my living room.

'Take a look out the window,' he instructed me. When I did, it was to see his familiar figure standing on the sidewalk directly below me. He waved, just to make sure I'd realised it was him.

'What are you doing here?'

'We need to talk, Summer. And I thought I could stand here and discuss things with you, or maybe we could do it the civilised way, and you could invite me up.' When I didn't immediately answer, he continued, 'You ran out on me this morning, and I didn't know why. Then I had the most interesting chat with my darling stepsister ...'

Oh God, he'd seen Heather. What had she said to him? My fingers gripped the phone so tightly my knuckles had gone white. 'OK, I'll let you in.'

I went over to press the door buzzer, still not sure I was doing the right thing. A minute later, Eddie knocked at the door. Taking a deep breath, praying this wouldn't turn ugly, I answered it.

'Summer.' Despite everything, the sight of him stopped me in my tracks. Like me, he'd left the Mallory dressed in the same outfit as the night before, and I couldn't help but think how handsome he looked in his tuxedo, hair rumpled and an expression on his face that mixed hurt with resolve. The way he regarded me made me all too aware that I wore nothing but the loosely belted robe.

'Eddie.' I clutched the robe a little tighter to myself. 'I'm sorry I left without saying goodbye, but I had to. I couldn't stay, not after what happened between us.'

He took a pace closer. 'You see, this is what I don't understand. What happened last night was that I had some of the greatest sex of my life, and I'm pretty sure you'd say the same. I made a connection to you like I've never made with anyone else, felt things I've never ...' He sighed, running a hand through his hair. 'And then you just up and leave without a word, like it didn't mean anything.'

Shaking my head, I grasped the sofa arm for support, gathering my strength for what I was about to say. 'Eddie, it meant more to me than you could ever know. But you'd said it was only going to be one night, just to make Heather think we were a real couple, and I couldn't do anything that would let myself believe we had more of a future than that.' Something he'd said about my leaving without a word struck home. 'But I didn't just leave – didn't you get my note?'

'Note? I didn't see any note.'

'Well, I left it on the nightstand.'

He rubbed his face. 'Now you say that, I do remember a piece of paper falling off the nightstand when I was scrabbling for the room key. I never thought to see what it was, and I didn't stop to check. I'd woken up to see you shutting the door on your way out. I stuck my head out into the corridor and called after you, but you couldn't have heard me.'

'The elevator came straight away. I must have been in it by that time.' I didn't mention that I thought I'd heard someone shout my name, but had dismissed the idea.

'Well, I got dressed as quick as I could, and went down to the lobby, hoping against hope that you might not have left. There was no sign of you, but that's when I bumped into Heather.'

'Oh yes, Heather.' I bit back what I really wanted to say about her as Eddie went on.

'Yeah, she told me she'd just seen you. Said she'd finally found out the truth about us. Of course, I thought you'd come clean about the fact we weren't dating, and I was preparing myself for whatever shit storm she was going to throw at me – and then she said she knew you didn't work on the *Reporter*, and that if you were lying about that, who knew what else you were lying about? Started telling me about the reputation you had on the *Reporter*, though where all that came from I don't know.'

'I'm sorry, Eddie. I didn't realise it, but my old boss was at the ball last night. She's a friend of Heather's, and she gave her all the ammunition she needed.'

'Believe me –' Eddie spread his hands in an expansive

gesture '– when it comes to my girlfriends, Heather doesn't need help in conducting a character assassination. She makes her mind up about them before she ever meets them. And that's why I told her I already knew you didn't work at the *Reporter*, since I'd been employing you at the bar for the best part of two months. And the reason I hadn't told her you were my barmaid was because I knew exactly how she'd tear you down for your choice of job and me for my choice of girlfriend.' Passion blazed in his eyes; he punched the sofa cushion with his fist.

'I bet she didn't take too kindly to that.' I could all too easily picture him and Heather, trading verbal blows with each other in the plush lobby of the Mallory Hotel. Had Phillip stepped in to back up his wife, like he had when she'd been chewing me out, or had he deferred to the younger man's strength and obvious self-assurance?

'To be honest, I was past caring by then,' he admitted. 'I told her it didn't matter what she thought. I loved you, I wanted to be with you more than any other woman I'd ever known, and nothing she said was going to make any difference to that.'

I didn't hear anything he said for a good few seconds after that, too busy digesting those last words. He'd told Heather he loved me. No "might be", no "think I'm falling" about it. When I tuned back in again, he was saying, 'There's something I ought to tell you about my stepsister. Maybe it'll help explain why she's got such a downer on everyone I date. I take it you met Phillip?'

'Uh-huh.' Not quite sure what the man had to do with all this, I listened, picking at the terry fabric of my robe, as Eddie continued.

'Heather started working for Phillip's firm straight out of business school, on one of these fast-track graduate programmes. She was always going to work her way to the top, whichever company took her on, but she caught Phillip's attention on a personal level too. And Heather was one of those girls who didn't have time for a relationship in school; she always claimed it would get in the way of her studies.'

I nodded. I'd been at college with girls like that. 'So Phillip was her first serious boyfriend?'

'Yeah, they were married less than a year after she started working for him. And don't get me wrong, he's a decent guy. But he's safe, conservative. I mean, I can't ever see him doing anything like fucking her up against a window with the drapes open.'

I blushed, the memory flooding back of how it had felt to have my breasts pressed against the cold glass as Eddie's cock pistoned into me hard from behind. Eddie was right; Phillip didn't strike me as the type to initiate any kind of wild monkey sex.

'And I think there's a part of Heather that sees me having all this fun, never thinking about settling down, and realises what she's missed out on – and she resents me for it. That's why she likes to make trouble for me, whether she's aware of it or not. You know, it's not all been bad, because I think she may have driven away a couple of chicks who might have spelled trouble for me down the line in one way or another.' Eddie's voice dropped, and he stared at his hands, as though not quite sure how to phrase his next statement. 'But I'm really, really hoping her bitterness hasn't driven you away from me, because I look at you, and I start to think that settling down, and getting to know another person just as well as I know myself, might not be such a bad thing after all.'

'Eddie, I don't know what to say.' Everything was beginning to make more sense, but I still wasn't convinced I hadn't ruined everything by leaving his room at the Mallory the way I had.

He took my hand, clutched it to his chest, close to his heart. 'Say you feel the same way I do. Say you could see yourself spending more than one night with me.'

I couldn't speak, could only nod. I'd feared that Eddie had been swept away by the excitement of the situation, and that in the cold light of morning he'd remember he'd only wanted me to play a temporary part. Now I knew he wanted more than that, I could give myself to him without reservation.

His mouth came down on mine, and the way he smiled made me wonder if he could taste frosting on my lips. We kissed for long moments, growing short of breath as our tongues battled and explored. Eddie's hands reached into the front of my robe, moving over the contours of my breasts, my nipples stiffening at his touch as I moaned into his mouth. I let him push the robe off my shoulders completely, unbelting it so it fell open. He didn't even bother to remove his jacket, just got down before me on the floor, spreading my legs wide to give him access to my pussy. Being so naked and open before him filled me with a strange mixture of vulnerability and power, and I couldn't resist stroking a lazy finger along my crease, hearing Eddie's tortured groan as I touched where he so clearly wanted to. He grabbed my hand, putting it to his lips and licking it clean, then bent to run his tongue over my sex lips, tasting the dewy moisture that had gathered there. His hot breath sighed at the entrance to my cunt, and I could only moan and clutch fistfuls of his hair, holding him in place as he lapped away.

When he briefly darted his tongue inside me, wreaking glorious havoc with the sensitive places there, I gripped at the edges of my robe and squealed in pleasure. If he never stopped licking me out, it would be too soon. Heather might be a royal pain in the ass, driven by her own selfish agenda, but by insisting that Eddie attend the Masquerade Ball and take a partner with him, she had inadvertently brought us together.

Marvelling at the bizarre way things worked out sometimes, I surrendered to the power of Eddie's tongue work, lost in an orgasm that made colours dance behind my tightly shut eyelids. When I opened my eyes again, it was to see Eddie stripping out of his tux.

'You taste so good,' he said, 'but I really need to be inside you.' As he spoke, he was kicking off his shoes, easing down his underwear. Again, once he was naked he went hunting for a condom in the folds of his wallet, coming up triumphant for a second time.

'Let me,' I said, pushing him back on to the sofa. With fingers that trembled despite myself, I smoothed the cool latex down over his hot, hard cock. I straddled him, poising myself over his shaft and waiting a moment, letting the anticipation build, before slowly sinking down on to that thick, fleshy rod. My cunt welcomed him, settled round him like a glove, holding him tight. As I began to ride him, he reached up to cup my breasts in his hands, rubbing my nipples with his thumbs. No words were spoken as I shifted up and down on his cock; our eyes were locked together as I demonstrated my need for him. Being on top gave me the chance to set the pace, moving in a rhythm designed to suit us both.

Faster and faster I ground myself down on him, feeling the friction, the heat between us rising as we fucked. Waves of pleasure rolled through my belly, and at last Eddie's hips rose to meet my thrusts. With a long drawn out groan, he shuddered and came.

'God, Summer, I love you,' he murmured, when he was able to speak again.

'And I love you too,' I just about managed to reply, before a second orgasm, stronger than my first, caught me up and swept me away.

When it was all over, we just held each other tight, whispering soft words that indicated how deeply we'd come to feel about each other, even in the few short weeks I'd been working for Eddie. I nestled in the crook of his arm, thinking just how close I'd come to losing this wonderful man and wondering how I could have been quite so stupid as to let fears of things that might never happen stop us from being together.

Somewhere close by, my cell phone trilled. It took me a moment to locate it, still in the pocket of my coat, which I'd thrown over the back of the sofa. I caught the call just before my voicemail kicked in.

'Hello?' I sounded more than a little blissed-out.

'Summer,' Delia said, worry in her tone. 'I got your call, honey. You sounded upset. Is everything OK?'

I glanced at Eddie where he was slumped beside me, his shaggy hair falling over his face and his chest rising and falling in the slow, shallow motions that indicated impending sleep. 'Oh yes,' I assured her. 'Everything's way better than OK.'

Epilogue

EDDIE WAS IN THE shower, singing off-key as he soaped himself down. I lay curled in the bedsheets, wondering whether to go join him and see if he needed any help scrubbing his back. Or maybe I'd just roll over and sleep a little longer; after all, it wasn't like I had to get up and go back to my own place.

After he'd poured his heart out the morning after the Masquerade Ball, telling me exactly how he felt about me, I knew I couldn't walk out on my job at his bar – or him – the way I'd planned to. He was right; it wasn't important what Heather, or anyone else, thought about us. We weren't pretending to be crazy about each other; we really were, and that was the only thing that mattered.

That night, we'd announced to the other staff that we were dating; Penny squealed in delight and hugged us both, while Rudy's reaction was a simple, 'What took you so long?'

And now, six months later, I'd at last taken the plunge and moved in with Eddie. It still didn't quite seem real; even Delia couldn't believe I'd made such a grown-up decision, though the fact my landlord had been making noises about getting the builders in to start remodelling the property might have forced my hand a little.

Looking at him as he emerged from the bathroom, towel wrapped round his waist and his hair tousled and shower-damp, I couldn't doubt I'd done the right thing.

He smiled down at me. 'Hey, sleepyhead, rise and shine. I was thinking we could go get breakfast at the diner on the corner of Hudson. I'm in the mood for blueberry pancakes with plenty of butter and maple syrup. What do you say?'

'Sounds like a great idea.'

He bent and kissed me, a kiss that lingered, threatening to turn into something deeper. As it still did every time we kissed, lust for him threatened to overwhelm me. In Eddie, I'd found a man who was as straightforward as they came, who saw no need to mask his feelings, or his desires, and who loved me as completely as I loved him. And what more could a girl want?

Apart from blueberry pancakes, of course ...

Seducing Mr Storm
by Poppy Summers

Chapter One

SUSANNA SEYMOUR STARED OUT at the magpies and sparrows feeding on the crumbs of bread scattered over the lawn and wished she was outside with the birds. It was a glorious spring morning, blue sky chasing away the ragged clouds of last night's storm, green as far as the eye could see from the edges of the Seymour estate and into the wilds of the Yorkshire moors. Susanna often dreamt of clambering around the rocks and hiding in the long grass, buffeted by the wind and the rain, pursued by nature's elements. Ever since she left her teens, her parents had deemed her too old to play on the moors, too old since she reached the age of 27 to ever be married, firmly on the shelf and cast in the spinster role while they instead looked for a husband for 21-year-old Lucy.

It wasn't that there hadn't been offers for Susanna's hand before, but she had turned them all down flatly. It served her right for reading too many novels and thinking her own romantic hero might be out there somewhere. It had got her nowhere other than confined to her parents' house for the rest of her life.

Lucy's prospective suitor, their new neighbour at Rainton Grange, would call today to pay his respects. Having already asked around, Elizabeth Seymour knew he had an income of £20,000 a year and was thought of well in his usual circles in London. The Grange was somewhere to holiday for the rakish bachelor, and Mrs Seymour was keen to hook him for Lucy without preamble. All she had talked about in the six days since he had written to accept their lunch invitation was the rumour that the exotically named Elijah Storm was as arresting as his moniker.

Susanna couldn't care less. Mr Storm could go right to hell for all she gave a damn. She was sick of meeting Lucy's suitors and sick of having people look at her in pity for missing her chance. In all reality, she wasn't sure she cared about having a man. What did it matter when men such as those in the novels didn't exist anyway?

A commotion in the hall signalled the arrival of their guest, Lucy's little dog, Toby, yapping excitedly. Her mother gathered up her skirts and fled to a chair, arranging herself with deliberate boredom as though she had not just spent the last two hours gazing from the window in anticipation.

Susanna lingered apathetically behind, prepared to be little more than disdainful towards whichever fop stepped through the door. The door opened, Richard bowed and announced loudly, 'Mr Elijah Storm,' and Susanna's knees almost buckled as an angel fallen from heaven entered their parlour.

He was perhaps in his late 30s and tall, almost a head taller than her father at about six feet, and so well made! He wore a black suit with white linen, the lace at his throat and cuffs understated and neat. His body almost strained the velvet of his frock coat and breeches, his shoulders broad, his thighs strong and ...

Susanna's gaze halted halfway down his body, drawn magically in to the apex of his thighs. Good God, what was that down his breeches? Her cheeks turned scarlet as she saw the bulge at his crotch, the material hugging cock and balls greedily. She swallowed, her eyes flying to his stunning face and finding ice-blue eyes fixed on hers, dancing with amusement at her awe.

Susanna swallowed, pressed a hand behind her against the glass to hold herself upright. His perfect face was almost pretty, even though there was nothing effeminate about him. His bone structure, the curve of his sensual, somewhat sardonic lips, and the sooty lashes over his crystal eyes. His skin was lightly tanned, as though he spent plenty of time outdoors in rough, masculine pursuits despite his class. Scandalously, he wore neither wig nor ribbon, his hair black as a raven's wing and cut close to his neck. Susanna saw her mother perusing him with shock and awe as she held out her hand to be kissed.

Elijah Storm turned his attention to his hosts. He bent low over Elizabeth Seymour's hand, his lips just about grazing it, before shaking Edward Seymour's hand firmly. The way her mother simpered, it was obvious which of her daughters was intended for their neighbour, as she introduced a giggling, blushing Lucy and Elijah once more air-kissed Susanna's sister's hand.

Elizabeth threw Susanna a cool, impatient look, gesturing angrily behind their guest's back, and she stepped forward on unsteady legs. Elijah turned her way, amusement still lighting those startling eyes as though he'd read every one of her impure thoughts about his fine physique and known exactly on which area of his anatomy her gaze lingered.

She tripped over the edge of the rug as she walked forward and his hand instantly shot out and steadied her, catching her forearm with long, delicate fingers, the heat of which seemed to scorch her. She blushed as hard as her sister, disentangled herself demurely, and bent her head, presenting her hand and avoiding his gaze. His lips came down to make deliberate contact with her knuckles, and she stifled a gasp, a little throb of something between her legs startling her. She stepped back, keeping her head bent as though in subservience, not daring to make eye contact.

They went through to the dining room for lunch, and Susanna found herself seated opposite Mr Storm. She stared down at her plate while she tried to order her scattered thoughts. Certainly she had noticed men's bodies before, but none had ever been quite so direct and obvious as Elijah Storm. He seemed to wear his very sexuality on the outside for anyone to see. Even her father was clearly intimidated by the man's virile masculinity, his forceful presence in the room and unique looks.

Susanna had only seen one man naked before, and that was one of their servants, Cuthbert, who she'd discovered bathing in the river to the east of the lodge. Wandering in the woods on a summer day, she had heard splashing and caught flashes of sun-kissed skin through gaps in tree branches. Startled, embarrassed, she had noticed a pile of clothing on the ground and stopped, looking at the underwear on top. She'd cast around before she had delicately fingered the rough, woollen material, imagining Cuthbert, a tall, strapping lad of 19, wearing it. Then, not quite ashamed yet at her forthrightness, she had deliberately ducked behind a tree and spied on him.

He was tanned all over apart from his milk-white backside. Her gaze lingered on the lean cheeks of his bottom, caught a glimpse of the sac swinging between his legs before he pushed off, and started to swim. As he spread his legs, she saw cock and balls dangling in the water, and she clutched at the tree trunk, gaze rooted in fascination.

Cuthbert swam for some minutes, then he stood upright and waded briskly out of the river. Susanna's jaw dropped open. The equipment between his legs was heavy, his cock turgid, half-hard and thick, surrounded by a dense, dark bush. His balls were big, furry, swinging enthusiastically as he climbed from the water.

Susanna swallowed, crept away through the trees as quietly as she could. She made it back to the house and up to her room with her heart pounding. Once locked in her bedchamber, she paced. She felt too hot. Her dress constricted her bosom, her stockings squeezed her thighs.

She stripped quickly. Looking down, she saw her nipples were rigid against her chemise. She pulled the straps down, rubbed a fingertip lightly over one peak and gasped at the answering sensation that shot down her stomach to her groin. God in heaven, what was happening to her? She throbbed between her legs, an ache of need she could not identify. Peeling down her linen drawers, she perched on the edge of the bed and spread her thighs, looking in the glass. She was swollen, glistening between her distended lips. She touched the bud at the apex of her sex, felt how hard it was, and then rubbed it up and down, feeling wetness seeping from her core.

She knew men touched themselves this way, had even heard salacious talk of special clubs where men went to masturbate and compare their organs, but this ... Surely this would send her straight to hell? At that moment, she hoped Lucifer himself welcomed her. Preferably naked and hard, with a cock the very equal of Cuthbert's. With enthusiasm, she rubbed herself harder while burying one finger into the wet chamber of her cunny, slickly fucking the tight hole. God, it was good; it was like nothing else ever. She frigged away at herself until she felt it coming.

A climax that shook her entire body, made her cry out in shocked ecstasy before she fell back onto the bed, barely conscious.

That was the first time she had come to sexual awareness, courtesy of Cuthbert, so now she knew all too well why her drawers were wet as she sat looking at Elijah Storm across the dining table. Oh God, let this dinner be over soon so she could hurry away and pleasure herself over her new neighbour.

She reddened at her thoughts, kept her head dipped as she sensed the man's gaze on hers. Her mother chattered brightly, drawing Lucy into the conversation, where Susanna's sister showed how empty-headed and truly idiotic she was. But Susanna guessed it was better that than socially redundant and on the shelf like herself. She knew which one appealed more to men. Obviously they didn't like their wives to think for themselves. Susanna liked bird-watching, walking, and reading. She doubted this was compatible with the ideas modern men had about women.

Elijah Storm, though, to her surprise, was somewhat dry and dour. While charming, he had a line in barely decent remarks about this or that Lord who had lost his fortune to gambling or opium, scandalous tales of wives embroiled in affairs with earls or even their groomsmen.

She found herself listening in fascination, watching Elijah lift his wine glass to his sensual mouth, his Adams's apple bobbing as he swallowed. She wasn't sure if her neighbour was making the right impression on her mother. Was he altogether *too* modern for Elizabeth? She hid a smirk behind a napkin and thought she saw Elijah's gaze flicker over hers, a smile curling around his lips.

Elizabeth steered the conversation towards the up and coming ball at Bennet Hall, the social event of late spring every year. Susanna had been attending since she was 16. Every year she was courted by a string of foppish dandies with lace handkerchiefs who stood on her toes at the dance and asked her to ride with them in their carriage next day. She had always refused. None of them had ever captured her imagination, not even under the influence of wine and song, much to her mother's chagrin.

'When is it?' Elijah asked politely. 'At present, I am unsure when I will return to London.'

Her mother looked panicked. 'Next Friday,' she said. 'Surely you will make special dispensation to attend?'

Elijah looked amused. 'I have yet to be invited.'

'My dear Mr Storm,' Elizabeth said. 'If a man of your standing in the community –' for this, Susanna read "a purse of your size" '– has yet to be invited, then I would take carte blanche upon myself to attend regardless and hold my head up against the snub!' She flushed at her outburst and signalled Cuthbert for some water.

A sly smile curved Elijah's lips. 'Why, Mrs Seymour, you're a lady after my own heart. I've ridden into more social occasions uninvited than I've had hot dinners.'

Susanna rolled her eyes as her mother almost melted into a puddle at the great man's flattery. She couldn't help wondering if Mr Storm had a certain reputation that caused people to shun him socially. No doubt he was a ladies' man; with that physique he must be bedding any number of lovers. Poor Lucy. What a shock she would get when they were married.

Elizabeth rubbed her hands. 'That's settled then. Next week at Bennet Hall. And I hope you will give my daughter the privilege of first dance.'

Elijah's gaze flickered instantly to Susanna and her cheeks flamed, while Elizabeth looked appalled.

'*Lucy*, my dear Mr Storm. It is Lucy to whom I wish to

present you at the ball.'

Elijah dabbed at the corners of his mouth with his napkin. 'Of course,' he said demurely while looking at Susanna from under his heavy lashes.

Susanna escaped upstairs finally, with a last kiss to her hand from their neighbour as he went to take a turn around the grounds with her father. Oh God help her, she had never been so stricken with lust over a man in all of her 27 years. She slammed her bedroom door and turned the key, and then she hurried to lift her complicated skirts, piling them around her as she sat on the end of the bed with legs splayed.

She moaned at the first touch of her swollen flesh beneath her underwear. This was what Elijah Storm had done to her with his teasing little looks and smiles and that body made for sin. He had made her wet and hard and aching. She closed her eyes and imagined it was his large hand between her legs, bringing her to the sweetest of climaxes, and she came, those ice-blue eyes behind hers as she shuddered and writhed on the bed.

Chapter Two

SUSANNA HAD TRIED TO rationalise her instant obsession with Elijah Storm away by the time she took to the grounds for a long walk two days later. The birds sang overhead as she wandered deep into the woods, and the sun shone sporadically through the thick canopy of tree branches. Her pretty little boots had just been mended after she had worn them out walking, and they were sturdy as she lifted her skirts to climb over rocks and tree roots.

The woods meandered down to the melodic river, its little waterfall at one end swollen with the recent rainwater and filtering down through the trees musically. The river wound all the way from the Seymour estate to their new neighbour's, then on down to the ocean, a mile away on the coast. Even from here one could smell the scent, and Susanna suddenly longed to swim in the sea. Never mind, the river would do as well. If it wasn't too cold, she could remove her boots and stockings and paddle in the shallow water. She grinned at the fit her mother would have if she knew.

Brushing through the trees, she came upon the river and stopped dead as a sound hit her ears. She wasn't alone. Coming from somewhere up by the riverbank she heard grunts and moans in a male voice that lifted the hair at the back of her neck and set goosepimples up and down her arms.

Susanna crept closer, staying behind tree trunks. He was there, in the clearing, holding onto an oak tree firmly with one palm, breeches pulled down around his thighs, and his other hand wrapped around his thick, straining shaft.

Elijah Storm, self-pleasuring, in the middle of the day, out in the open, on *her* land!

Her mouth gaping and her heart pounding, Susanna stealthily moved closer, peeping from behind a willow trunk. Never in her wildest imaginings had she dreamt of seeing anything so exciting, so – arousing as this.

She stared at Elijah's manhood, an iron rod of immense proportions, thick, long, and made to satisfy. Susanna shuddered. She pressed her thighs together as a rush of moisture dampened her drawers. Elijah was as beautiful beneath his breeches as she had imagined. A neat thatch of dark hair showed through the opening to his underwear. He groaned, tugging harder and harder at his cock, its rosy head leaking a pearl drop, his fingers tight and his thighs shaking.

His other hand dipped into his linen underwear. He pulled his heavy sac free and she saw his balls were like two ripe plums, the skin pink and smooth, so different from the hairy ones she had seen on Cuthbert. Did he shave? And who for? His women? She stared at his tight, bulging sac. For a moment she imagined running her tongue over it, feeling the soft, pink skin before sucking each ball into her mouth. Oh God, it was too much. Her thoughts drove her to the very edge of lust. What about that cock? What would it feel like if he drove it deep inside her, splitting her apart and filling her full?

Susanna sagged against the tree, clutching tight, seconds away from lifting her skirts to seek her own pleasure. Still her gaze remained riveted on Elijah, who hefted and squeezed his balls with one hand while he worked his cock furiously hard with his other. He panted, mouth open, eyes squeezed shut, and then he let out a long, guttural growl that Susanna nearly answered with a moan of her own. He shot his load, thick ropes of white semen splattering the tree trunk in seemingly never-ending spurts, before he steadied himself a moment, breathing hard.

After a few seconds, he plucked a large leaf from the tree and wiped off his soiled hand. Then he tucked his equipment back into his confining breeches and fastened up. Swiftly, he strode away down river.

Susanna peeked from behind the tree until he was lost in the distance. With her heart still racing, she stepped out into the clearing, approaching the oak Elijah had been leaning against. There it was, his seed coating the rough tree bark. Susanna glanced around. Then she dipped the tip of her forefinger into one of the pools of white, brought it to her mouth, and tasted Elijah Storm.

She closed her eyes at the heady essence of him. Mr Storm was going to drive her firmly out of her mind; she was sure of it.

Susanna tried her best to cope with her mother and sister's feverish plans for the ball at Bennet Hall for the next few days. The day loomed large over all other considerations and trips to town were undertaken, gowns and accessories ordered, jewels and shoes cleaned.

Susanna chose a demure black number because she knew it suited her hourglass figure. Cut low at the front with skirts of stiff, watered silk, her mother considered it dowdy even though Susanna thought it sophisticated and sexy to some degree. Next to Lucy's over-the-top peach and lace number, with its gigantic ruffles that probably wouldn't fit in the carriage, and plunging cleavage, she guessed there was no competition for ludicrous dress of the season, although the Farnham sisters from Tinsley Lodge were usually a hard act to beat.

The evening arrived and the family crammed itself into their carriage and set off down the sweeping driveway to the road. Susanna was nervous of seeing Elijah again now she'd witnessed him doing that most private of things. Perhaps he would see her guilt on her face? Perhaps it would ruin Lucy's chances with him. Not that Susanna seriously wanted her sister to marry her depraved neighbour. What sort of life would Lucy lead with a man who masturbated on the riverbank and told scandalous tales at dinner? A hot flash of emotion flared in her belly, tightening it into knots, and she identified it reluctantly as jealousy. Please God, don't let Mr Storm fall in love with Lucy when he could have me ...

She laughed at her ludicrous thoughts.

The grounds were heaving with carriages discharging guests dripping in jewels and finery, and Elizabeth linked Lucy's arm as they went inside, leaving Susanna to bring up the rear with her father. The vast hall was decorated in sumptuous style, a long corridor leading them into the ballroom, a band playing busily at one end and the dance floor full of couples.

Susanna recognised ladies of her acquaintance, most of them married to men she had turned down. She watched the stilted steps of the dance and wished she was anywhere but here. Preferably lying down in the woods watching birds clandestinely. Failing that, watching Mr Storm wanking clandestinely.

Lucy squealed delicately. She gripped her mother's arm and Elizabeth straightened up, thrusting out her ample bosom as a swathe of interested observers parted to reveal Elijah Storm.

If Susanna had thought swooning was remotely proper and not for simpering girls, she might have done so when she saw Elijah in his stiff white linen and cravat, his dapper black suit, his hair all glossy and freshly trimmed so it was even shorter, to the furious whispers of those all around him.

A helpless heat rose over Susanna's cheeks as she perused his godly countenance, fighting not to let her gaze drop to that part of him that fascinated her so.

'Miss Seymour –' He greeted Lucy, bowing low over her gloved hand. 'Mrs Seymour.' Again his lips swooped over Elizabeth's knuckles. Susanna wasn't wearing gloves and her palms were damp. She blotted her hand on her dress and held it out. Elijah took it, his cool fingers wrapping around it delicately, ice-blue eyes unblinkingly on hers as he once more kissed her hand, lips actually making contact. He smiled, a secretive smile that seemed to read her mind and her heart, and then he addressed Mr Seymour, suggested they furnish the ladies with some wine. The two of them wandered off towards the end of the room, leaving Lucy and Elizabeth giggling like schoolgirls and Susanna praying for the night to end soon.

She listened to her sister and mother plot and scheme over the availability of Mr Storm and his purse. Her heart sank as a waiter returned carrying four glasses of wine and, on the periphery of her vision, Elijah danced past with Sarah Farnham in his arms.

Lucy's mouth dropped open. Her big brown eyes swam with tears. 'Oh, fie!' exclaimed Elizabeth, bringing her daughter's head to her bosom while the waiter hovered nervously with the wine.

'He's a rake,' Susanna said calmly. 'I thought you knew that, Lucy. He isn't suitable husband material.'

Only suitable masturbation material, she added silently, angry at the cad for breaking her sister's heart. Hadn't he virtually promised the first dance to Lucy? She took her wine from the tray and took an unladylike swig. Alcohol seemed to be the only way to get through tonight.

The four of them had moved to some seats at the edge of the dance floor when Elijah finished his dance. He glanced in their direction, quickly assessed the hostile looks and moved along, although his gaze lingered on Susanna. She wasn't sure she had ever felt warmth toward this man but any feeling she had once been susceptible to had now vanished, replaced with cold anger. Damn him to hell. She finished her wine and excused herself to take some air.

The house was stiflingly hot that mild spring evening. She ducked into the library, glanced around the brightly lit room, and crossed the floor to unlatch a window, breathing great lungfuls of the sweet night air with relief.

She heard the door click shut behind her. She spun around to see Elijah Storm smiling at her. 'Miss Seymour, what a lovely surprise.'

Warily, she regarded him as he approached. Propping himself on the edge of the desk, he crossed his long legs at the ankle, stretched out, his frock coat falling open to show the bulge beneath the velvet. God in heaven, he was going to be the death of her.

She swallowed, tried to keep her eyes on those crystal ones of his. 'What do you want?'

He regarded her, head cocked. 'You're angry with me.'

'You humiliated my sister.'

'I did?'

Susanna clenched her fist. 'Don't play games. You promised her first dance.'

Elijah looked amused. 'I don't recall.'

'Damn you, sir!'

Elijah lifted a brow. 'Really, Miss Seymour. I should wash your mouth out with soap and water.' His smile was sly. 'And then put you over my knee.'

She flushed violently. 'You should stay away from my family, Mr Storm. You're not the sort of gentleman we wish to entertain.'

His face darkened. 'Is that so? Do you consider yourself better than me, Miss Seymour?'

'You know what I'm talking about. Your less than gentlemanly behaviour.'

Elijah stood upright suddenly and strode forward so he towered over her. He purred into her ear in a loud whisper. 'Miss Seymour, I would no more wish to be wed into your common, lowly family that I would want to wed a man. In fact, I would *prefer* to wed a man. A strapping stable boy with a good behind.'

Susanna's jaw dropped. She couldn't countenance any more of his insulting manner. When she tried to brush past him, he caught her arm hard. 'You, however,' he said silkily, 'are a different matter entirely. You have all the spunk your sister didn't get.'

Susanna trembled in his grip. "You, sir, have all the spunk, from what I saw the other day", she wanted to retort, but that would surely drop her to his level. His wide grin, showing his perfect, pearly teeth, suggested he read her mind anyway.

'Indeed,' he said, pressing her back against the window, a thigh thrusting between hers. 'You like to look, do you not? I like that in a woman.'

She stared, quivering like a trapped bird, her face growing hotter and hotter. 'I don't understand,' she tried to bluff her way out.

Elijah eased forward so she felt an unmistakeable

erection against her hip and gasped aloud. 'You like to watch,' he repeated. 'A man, pleasuring himself.'

Her mouth opened in a perfect O of astonishment at being caught out this way. She stammered, looking for an excuse where there was none. Elijah laughed. 'It made me spend extra hard to know you watched me, little one. Perhaps I can give you another private show now, seeing as you've girded my loins good and proper this evening.' He let her go and stepped back, wrenching open the fastenings of his breeches.

'Sir!' she tried to protest as all her dreams came true.

Chapter Three

ELIJAH GRINNED AS HE hefted his tool from his breeches. It was swollen with arousal, and as he handled it fondly with practised fingers, it grew harder still. 'Come now, my lady,' he said. 'Don't act as though you've never seen this before.'

Susanna cowered back against the window, hand over her mouth. Her thighs shook. Between them, she was damp. She stared at the hypnotic sight of Elijah caressing his manhood. She could clearly see the little slit at the head of his cock, how it opened as he tugged to let a pearly drop roll down his shaft. Elijah caught it with his finger. To her utter scandal, he then sucked the taste off, just as she had done at the tree, laughing when he saw her expression.

'Oh Miss Seymour,' he said. 'Of course I want a lady to act like a lady, but not in private. When I'm alone with a woman I want her to tell me what she wants. I want her to be dirty, so dirty it makes my blood boil.'

She looked from his prick back up to his cool blue eyes. 'What *I* want, Mr Storm,' she said icily, 'is for you to let me go.'

He laughed. 'Am I holding you prisoner? What exactly would people say if they knew you were behind an unlocked door with a man who stroked himself for your attentions? Your reputation would be ruined.'

Susanna stalked forward, heart in her mouth, palm

raised to slap his vile face. He caught her hard by the arm before she could touch him, pulled her against the length of his muscled body, cock pressing against her gown, leaving marks.

'Now, if you were less of a lady,' he said in a harsh whisper, 'for sure I would bend you over this desk, lift your skirts, and give you a taste of what you so crave. But I find anticipation to be part of the fun, and I know soon you'll be begging me for it, Miss Seymour. At that time, I'll be happy to service your three holes any way you require.'

Susanna's mouth dropped open in disbelief. *Three* holes? 'You scoundrel!' she hissed.

'Aye,' Elijah said. 'A scoundrel who might have met his match.' He pressed his lips to her temple and she shuddered at the velvet touch. He gave a low groan, increasing the friction to his cock so he tugged madly. 'Now, where would you have me spend?'

Susanna jerked away quickly, anxious he was about to stain her gown. He merely grinned, eyes twinkling, cock rosy and straining, about to spurt. She felt her cunny clench with sudden, violent need, and bit her lip hard.

Elijah looked about him. Then he grabbed the lace handkerchief from the sleeve of her gown and held it close to the end of his cock as he gasped, bucking his hips. Susanna should have been outraged but she was too aroused. She looked at his flushed face, at the gleam of sweat on his top lip, and thought he was never more beautiful in that moment. She dropped her gaze in time to see the semen spurt from his rod, soaking the delicate lace over and over again. Elijah gave a satisfied sigh and wiped the last drops on the handkerchief. Then he folded up the little square into a neat, wet parcel and handed it to her. 'Thank you, my dear, it was a pleasure.'

Susanna handled the soiled lace gingerly, staring at him as he fastened up quickly. Elijah winked at her and slipped through the door, leaving her standing there alone.

It was a long time before Susanna rejoined her family. Mad with arousal, she slipped out through the window and walked through the warm, fragrant grounds. Holding the wet handkerchief, she pressed it to her nose and then her mouth, licking his seed from it. She both despised and wanted the man in equal measures. He seemed to see right inside her and know what his teasing did to her, how she needed to be taught pleasure by him. She knew he was the only one to do it.

As she walked through a secluded copse, noises from the other side of the trees stopped her in her tracks. She heard heavy breathing, the rustling of clothing, and then a low, guttural groan from a man. Trying not to move a muscle, Susanna pushed aside one branch to look into the clearing beyond. It was woman on her knees, gown and chemise pulled down to bare her heaving breasts, while a man stood above her, shoving his cock down her throat.

Susanna put a hand over her mouth but didn't draw back, riveted by the sight. There was clearly no forcing going on. The woman sucked on the man's tool eagerly while he pumped his hips, groaning; one of her hands disappeared into the folds of her gown, moving busily. Oh God. She wondered why Elijah hadn't attempted to put Susanna on her knees that evening. She knew deep down she would have sucked him with such gusto he would have exploded in minutes. She couldn't think of anything she wanted to do more at that moment than have Elijah's throbbing manhood in her mouth, hers to do with as she wanted. Stifling a soft moan, she worked a hand under her gown, into her soaked drawers, finding her slit slippery and open. She rubbed at her hard bud quickly, using her other hand over her mouth to stifle the gasps and groans she longed to spill forth as she worked her needy flesh.

The man had pulled his gleaming cock from the woman's mouth. He rested it in the valley of her cleavage and bucked forward; his partner encouraged him, pressing her large breasts together with her hands so he had the perfect chute in which to masturbate. Susanna stared, the eroticism of this scenario driving her on further. Both the man and the woman moaned in unison and the sound sent prickles down her spine and straight to her groin where her finger worked in a blur, rubbing so she knew she'd be sore, but not caring, not when she was so close. The man shot his load at that moment, creaming the woman's breasts, and his lover flung her head back, moaning, body shaking as clearly she climaxed too under her own hand.

Susanna let go. Her head fell back as she convulsed, trembling violently, frigging until she couldn't take any more. She eased herself back onto the grass with a soft bump and laid there, legs splayed and skirts in disarray, her heart pounding. On the other side of the trees were soft voices and laughter, then kisses, and then the couple retreated, leaving silence. Susanna lay in no rush to move.

To her horror, as she gained the corridor to the ballroom, Sarah Farnham fell into step with her, her ostentatious pink satin gown like some gigantic puffed-up meringue.

'Did you perchance see my dance partner, Mr Elijah Storm?' she questioned, giddy and breathless.

'Yes,' said Susanna sourly and wondered what it was about herself that made Elijah want to wank in front of her but not treat her to a dance.

'For sure he dances like an angel. I've heard it said he has an income of 20 thousand a year.'

'Is the size of his purse the only thing of interest to you?' Susanna said before she could stop herself.

Sarah's gaze darted to hers in astonishment, then a sly smirk curled around her lips. 'Why no, dear Susanna, I've heard it said the size of other things is more than a match for Mr Storm's purse.' She giggled as Susanna flushed, a hot flash of arousal darting to her recently sated groin as she thought of how she could verify such tales.

'Indeed,' she said with as much disinterest as she could muster. 'It's whether he knows what to do with it, though, isn't it?'

This time it was Sarah who blushed. 'Susanna,' she purred, 'you're positively indecent.' She linked arms with Susanna. 'I love it.'

For the first time, Susanna looked beyond the coquettishness and outrageous gowns and sensed a kindred spirit where she had never thought to look. She smiled tentatively. 'He's a wicked rake, Sarah, but he knows how to make a woman's heart flutter.' And her other parts, she added silently.

'Indeed. I would have to make sure one night with him would be worth being ruined for ever, though.'

Susanna's heart sank. She said nothing further.

They made it back to the ballroom, where Susanna discovered Lucy had found a young man to dance with and Elizabeth looked less like she was sucking lemons. Sarah rejoined her sillier younger sister and Susanna sat beside her mother, surveying the room.

'Perhaps you would care for a dance with Captain Westby?' Elizabeth suggested. 'He has looked your way more than once.'

Susanna shook her head. 'I'm tired.' Captain Westby was a fop of the highest order with a penchant for liquor, cards and – her mother would swoon to know it – other men. Susanna didn't care either way, but ... Her thoughts trailed off suddenly as she saw Elijah Storm leaning casually against the opposite wall, gaze fixed on hers. Susanna glanced around quickly, caught Captain Westby admiring her yet again, and gave him a shy smile in return. For the moment, he suited her purposes admirably. He soon took the hint and approached her.

'Miss Seymour, you look radiant tonight,' he said, bowing low over her hand. 'If I may have the honour?'

'You may,' Susanna said coolly as her mother darted a look of confusion at her. She rose, holding the Captain's hand all the way to the dance floor before waiting patiently for the new waltz to start. Her partner gripped her close, possessive arm around her waist. She threw Elijah a withering look as they danced past him and saw the dark expression on his face. Was he jealous? Could it be possible? Surely he'd merely been enjoying himself teasing her and didn't actually want her for himself? But what had he said in the library? "I know soon you'll be begging me for it, Miss Seymour. At that time, I'll be happy to service your three holes any way you require."

Her three holes pulsed just to recall his words. She bit her lip, holding her dance partner closer, once more feeling the never-ending arousal Elijah Storm was capable of inciting. She thought of that woman in the gardens again on her knees and imagined Elijah pushing her down to take his solid length between her lips, using her mouth for his pleasure.

Suddenly he moved, pushing himself off the wall and striding across the dance floor with such purpose that Susanna trembled. 'If I may cut in,' he said to Captain Westby, his tone brooking no argument; moreover, he was six inches taller than the captain and considerably more muscular. Westby blustered a bit, looking somewhat embarrassed, then relinquished Susanna. Elijah gripped her by the waist and the hand and swept her away.

Breathless and quaking, Susanna almost tripped over her feet trying to keep up with his swift pace. The arm around her waist was like steel. His large hand splayed out over her lower back, fingers reaching to the cleft of her buttocks, resting tight.

Elijah didn't look at her. 'If you're trying to make me jealous, you little minx, it worked,' he said between his teeth.

She caught her breath. His hand slipped lower, fingers digging in so their heat seemed to burn her through layers of clothes. 'Sir,' she said frostily. 'If your hand strays any lower, I'll slap your impudent face in front of all these people.'

'Miss Seymour,' was his rejoinder, 'if you don't stop pressing yourself so suggestively against my aching prick, I'll be forced to throw you over the nearest table and have my way with you, and all these people be damned.'

Susanna gasped. She tried to pull away and he merely laughed, crushed her closer, thrusting his erection against her groin, grinding into her with every step of the dance. The blood pulsed between her legs. Her underwear was soaked, her nipples tight and bullet hard against her dress. She could barely think for her arousal.

'You bastard,' she hissed under her breath.

He chuckled, leant down to her ear. 'When you want me, just say the word,' he whispered. 'You know where I live.' As the music ended, he reached down, using her as cover to adjust himself in his breeches before he stepped back, bowed, and walked away, his arousal still obvious.

Susanna made her way back to her seat on shaking legs.

'Well,' Elizabeth said tartly. 'He could not shun poor

Lucy any more publicly if he tried.'

Susanna didn't speak. She didn't trust her voice.

Chapter Four

THE HOUSEHOLD WAS THROWN into uproar when an invitation to dinner from Elijah Storm arrived the following week. Mrs Seymour forgot her wrath and hurriedly took the sisters into town for a dress fitting. Susanna was reluctant to have a new gown for the rake, but was pressurised into a deep green silk number which matched her eyes and plunged deep over her ample breasts. With her dark hair pinned up, she admired her reflection in the mirror and shivered when she thought, against her will, about inflaming the passions of Elijah once more. What was wrong with her? Hadn't she decided he was a no-good womaniser and that she didn't stand a chance against Lucy? She knew his type. He would play with her, sully her purity, and then settle down with her sister into respectability. She clenched her fists when she thought of that scene in the library, of his wanton sexuality when dancing with her, and she burned at how she had allowed his liberties like a common courtesan. She was a woman who should be looking for a man to love and respect her, not play with her like this libertine. No longer would he be allowed to do this to her.

The driveway swept up to the grandest of houses and Lucy and Elizabeth chattered giddily as Rainton Grange came into view, a somewhat sinister mansion that loomed over its environs and came with the seemingly obligatory ravens perched on its turrets. Susanna couldn't think of a more apt place for Elijah Storm to reside. They were ushered inside by a stiffly liveried butler, their cloaks taken, shown into the drawing room, and offered glasses of wine.

Their host strolled in after a few moments and every female jaw in the room dropped at his uncommon beauty. For a man, he had far more than his share. He wore a velvet suit of the darkest violet, his linen and cravat black, emphasising his honeyed skin and crystal blue eyes. Even Susanna caught her breath. Elijah smiled at his captive audience and did the usual hand kissing, trying his best not to neglect Susanna's father, who currently looked as though he would rather be anywhere but here. Susanna knew just how he felt. As much as Elijah's very presence electrified her, she wished to be safe and sound back at home.

Elijah turned his stunning eyes on her. His gaze passed admiringly over the curves of her body in the green gown in a rather blatant way. She presented her hand reluctantly and saw his meaningful smile as his sensual mouth brushed her knuckles, sending sparks of desire throughout her whole body. Susanna snatched her hand away as quickly as she could. She gulped some wine, her cheeks flushing.

Elijah turned his attention to Lucy. 'I'd like to offer my humblest of apologies for missing my dance with you,' he said.

Susanna scowled as Lucy blushed and simpered. What the hell was he playing at? He'd snubbed her in favour of Susanna and Sarah and now wanted to make it up to her? Was that was this invitation was about? Was it simply to rub her nose in the fact she would never get anything more respectable from him than spectating on his self-pleasure? Oh God, how would she deal with this man as her brother-in-law? She would go completely to pieces.

Lucy tried to be cool in accepting his apology, but she was too much the gauche girl with him to bear him a grudge. Susanna wished her sister would make him work much harder for her affections, but then she could hardly talk: how hard had *she* made Elijah work for her that night in the library? Nonetheless, things had not actually gone far enough that he had ruined her reputation. It was not too late to have nothing more to do with him.

Elijah escorted Lucy and Elizabeth through to the large, gloomy dining room, one on each arm, leaving the elder Seymours trailing behind. Her father exchanged a glance with Susanna. Perhaps he knew her mind entirely. She wondered what he thought about welcoming Mr Storm to the family.

Candlelight flickered on Elijah's face as he sat at the head of the table, with his guests seated on either side. Soup was served as Lucy chattered about the social highlights of that year and what was to come. Elizabeth sat contentedly, her husband and elder daughter ignored, her attention wholly focused on the repartee between Elijah and Lucy. Susanna saw no chemistry between the couple, though. Elijah might have been attentive, even gently flirtatious, but his mind seemed to be elsewhere. It made her think again that his invitation was nothing more than a cruel trick. Did he really pretend interest in Lucy in order to spite Susanna?

She gulped her wine and wished an end to the evening. Elijah turned his incredible eyes on her and raked her insides with his sensuality. Damn it, he wouldn't let this spark between them rest until he had ruined her, she was sure of it. What was she going to do about dampening his ardour? She knew one thing would work. Something wild and dangerous. If she gave herself to him, he would lose interest. He would cast her off and then marry her sister. He would never reveal what they had done for the sake of his new family's honour, and she would be safe. She would also have experienced him just once and it would be more than enough of this man one could never hope to trust. Or even like.

She clenched her hands into fists below the table, gaze fixed on her plate, debating back and forth with herself. She could seduce him. She could make it clear she offered herself on condition he married Lucy. As she was beyond capturing a man now, why not sacrifice herself for her sister's and her mother's happiness? Who would know or care about her ruin? She lifted her head and caught Elijah's eye. He seemed puzzled and unsettled by the new determination he must have seen there. Perhaps the boot was on the other foot, finally.

She had decided.

After dinner Elijah suggested a turn around the garden. Everyone was surprised, the hour being late, but in early summer, twilight was still some while away. It was chilly nonetheless, fires burning in the grates of the gloomy house. Lucy and Elizabeth were keen, while Edward remained nursing a glass of port by the fire in the library. Susanna acquiesced reluctantly, knowing she had no choice if she was ever to manufacture some time alone with their host.

Donning cloaks, the ladies stepped onto the gravelled path with Elijah bringing up the rear. They strolled gently. He was a good guide, pointing out his prized flowers and shrubs, talking about the work that went into the garden. Work that, scandalously for Elizabeth, who believed servants should do everything, he took a large part in. The walk was a long one, down the sloped lawn to the woods beyond, where they could hear the river burbling gently and Susanna was reminded of their encounter the previous week. Elijah glanced at her with a smile, as though he read her thoughts. Steeling herself against her distaste, she looked back at him with what she hoped was a seductive expression. For a moment his face settled into a frown as he held her gaze. Then he arched a brow, clearly unsure as to the way the wind was now blowing. She couldn't blame him for being confused as to her about-turn.

A cry from Lucy tore their eye contact apart. She lay in a crumpled heap, having twisted her ankle stepping into a rabbit burrow. Elijah uttered an oath under his breath and bent to attend her while Elizabeth fussed wildly, wringing her hands. Susanna stood apart, watching as Elijah swept her distressed sister up into his arms and carried her quickly back to the house. The two women trailed behind, Elizabeth theatrically upset and Susanna thinking it was a great deal of fuss about nothing.

Elijah carried Lucy up the stairs to a guest bedroom. There Elizabeth lifted Lucy's skirts to show her ankles – a somewhat risqué gesture in front of Elijah, who acted as if he saw ladies' ankles all the time. Susanna had no doubt he did, and more.

'I'll send word to the doctor in the village,' Elijah said, striding from the room.

Elizabeth peeled Lucy's stocking down and revealed no bruising or swelling, a pointless trip for the doctor as far as Susanna could see. But clearly both her sister and mother were revelling in playing the helpless flowers in front of their host so who was she to spoil their fun?

She backed out of the room unnoticed and closed the door quietly, almost bumping into Elijah on the landing.

'I've sent a boy to fetch him,' he said.

Susanna shrugged. 'I'm not sure he's needed.'

'Neither am I,' Elijah said frankly, 'but I wouldn't risk your mother's wrath by not offering.' He gave her a conspiratorial smile.

Susanna didn't return it. She regarded him a moment. Now she had decided on her plan of action, she felt intense dislike for him, no matter that his proximity made her tremble.

'Mr Storm,' she said, holding his gaze. 'I wish to discuss something with you in private.'

He searched her eyes. She was convinced he knew, and would refuse her just to be contrary.

Then he stepped back, and spread his arm, indicating the guest bedroom behind them. Susanna entered quickly, taking in the plush surroundings, the four-poster bed, and the window overlooking the darkening garden. Elijah closing the door sounded thunderous. He walked into the centre of the room, standing on a Turkish rug.

'Well?'

Susanna clasped her hands together. Oh, she was stupid. What had ever possessed her to carry out this idea? Wouldn't Storm have her anyway, then disappear back to London without marrying her sister? She would ruin herself pointlessly. Nonetheless, she was fixed in her course.

She lifted her chin, aware of the great height difference between them and hoping he would come no closer. 'Sir,' she said. 'I wish you to marry my sister. I am here to take steps to assure it.'

Elijah arched a brow, looking amused. 'You are?'

'Yes.' Susanna took a deep breath, and then plunged into the abyss. She stalked across the room, slammed her hand against his broad chest, and marched him back.

Perhaps stunned by her forcefulness, he lifted his hands in surrender, and stepped back, his eyes losing their amusement as the back of his knees hit the bed and he sat down abruptly. Susanna sank instantly to her knees and pushed his muscular thighs apart. He didn't have to touch her, after all. She knew all men wanted this.

Elijah's mouth opened in a little O of shock. Was he really not used to women taking such a course with him or was it the fact of Susanna herself doing this that so astonished him?

She reached to his waist and virtually tore his breeches apart, finding him without underwear. Elijah gasped as the coiled length of his cock sprang free, slapping heavily against his belly, as hard as last time she had seen it.

The sight of it made her moisten between her legs. She grasped his prick around the base and it felt like silk sheathing steel. 'Susanna,' he said as she bent her head, but she ignored him. She opened her mouth and sucked him down as far as she comfortably could. Elijah let out a strangled moan. He grasped her head, plunging his fingers into the waves of her hair and dislodging the pins that held it up.

Susanna withdrew and slid down his iron rod again, slicking him with saliva, working her tongue over the head of his cock. The feel of him in her mouth was a startlingly pleasurable sensation. She couldn't believe how much his heavy length made her throb with illicit excitement. She drew back, letting him pop from her mouth, then she laved his shaft busily with her tongue, flicking it over the slit before sliding all the way down to his balls. She dug into his breeches to free his sac, then she cupped it in one hand, sucking on each ball in turn, leaving his scrotum wet and pink.

Elijah gave a deep groan. He gripped her shoulder with his other hand while continued to dishevel her hair, urging her head back to his cock, panting for breath when she swallowed him again.

Her breasts felt swollen, her nipples pressing rigidly against her gown. She felt ashamed that doing this to him aroused her so much, but why was she so surprised? After all, everything about him excited her; why wouldn't sucking his manhood drive her into a frenzy? She had exchanged the power here, though. From the man who had held her on a string as he masturbated in front of her, she had taken control, to have him at her beck and call, ruled by the organ all men were ruled by.

She looked up imperiously through her lashes as she sucked, making eye contact with him, seeing how flushed his face was, how he bit his lip so it was swollen and red.

The hand on her shoulder caressed the bare skin. He trailed it down to cup her breast through the silk of her gown and her corset. She knocked it away immediately. No. He couldn't touch her. She would never recover from this if he did.

'Susanna,' he gasped out as she sucked harder and faster. His cock swelled in her mouth and she realised he would achieve his end and she would have to swallow. His hand tightened on the back of her neck. His thighs trembled, and she shoved her hand up his shirt, feeling the taut convulsing of his hard abdominal muscles.

Elijah pushed her back suddenly, roughly. He grasped his cock, passed his hand vigorously down the shaft once, and held it, spurting, to the deep valley of her cleavage. Semen laced her breasts, trickled down between them to vanish beneath her gown. Susanna arched wantonly at the scalding flood, unbearably aroused by what he had done.

Elijah gave a groan of satisfaction. The sticky load covered every exposed part of her breasts and still dripped from the head of his cock. Daringly, she dipped her head once more and ran her tongue over the slit, tasting him.

He hissed, gripped her hair, and Susanna raised her head, fixing her eyes coldly on his.

'You will marry my sister now,' she said. 'Do you understand?'

It was soft murmur of surrender. 'Yes.'

Susanna stood. Elijah held his handkerchief out to her. She snatched it, mopped up as best she could, and tossed the scrap of lace back negligently at him, soaked. Then she tucked stray tendrils of escaped hair behind her ears and left Mr Elijah Storm sprawled on the bed, cock still hard and, for once, utterly mastered.

She closed the door and leant against it, heart roaring and underwear soaked. Oh God, that little escapade had only driven him further inside her, as deep as it was possible to get.

Chapter Five

THE DOCTOR DIAGNOSED A sprain, but Elizabeth was quite determined Lucy could not be moved that night. Edward, of course, couldn't leave the ladies in a strange man's home so the whole family had no choice but to stay. No wonder her father didn't trust Elijah with his daughters, Susanna thought as a servant led the way with a candle to her room for the night. Her father was shrewd enough to judge Elijah's character but not, perhaps, concerned enough to put a stop to his wife and daughters mingling with the man. Perhaps he was happy for them to make their own mistakes. And what mistakes had been made so far. Susanna looked around the cheerless room, crossing her arms over her chest. As soon as Elijah recovered his senses from having them sucked out through his cock, he would rescind his promise to marry Lucy and this would all have been for nothing. That much was obvious.

She undressed and hung her fine dress over the back of a chair, then washed using the jug of water and bowl on the dresser. She touched the still sticky patch on her cleavage and closed her eyes in remembrance. Elijah Storm's seed, spilled for her and her alone.

Susanna awoke to a soft tap on the door. 'Susanna, my dear?' Susanna called sleepily for her mother to come in. She struggled to sit up, tucking the fine covers under her arms, naked beneath them.

Her mother entered wearing a nightcap and nightgown, Susanna knew not from where. She perched on the edge of the bed, looking drained. 'Poor Lucy was up all night with such terrible pain. Perhaps you heard her cries?'

'No, mother, the walls are thick.' Susanna dipped her head in shame.

'Mr Storm was very good. He attended us personally. He has gone to dine now with your father but I have asked that Lucy and I take breakfast in our room.'

Susanna made no comment.

'I am sure this unfortunate accident has brought them closer together. I anticipate Mr Storm will propose soon. Perhaps even before he goes back to London.'

Susanna swallowed. 'Are you quite sure he is the man for Lucy?'

Elizabeth frowned at her and Susanna saw her own doubts in her mother's eyes before she could hide them. 'What do you mean?'

'You know what I mean. His reputation, his behaviour. I want my sister to have a faithful, loving husband. Don't you?'

Elizabeth blushed as though Susanna had accused her of selling her daughter to the highest bidder. 'But of course, my dear,' she blustered. 'She shall want for nothing with Mr Storm. She will be ingratiated into the very cream of social circles …'

'Is that enough?' Susanna interrupted softly.

Her mother's grey eyes turned icy. 'I shall send for you when we are ready to leave,' she said, getting up from the bed.

Susanna sank back against the pillow as the door closed. What was wrong with her that she had tried to talk her mother out of the marriage when she had already sacrificed herself for Lucy's sake? No, better that it go ahead, that Elijah take Lucy to London for good and she never had to look upon his face again and imagine him bestowing his favours on her sister.

To her discomfort, as Susanna walked down the corridor to the dining room she met with her father, who was hastening upstairs to see his wife and daughter. Her stomach rumbled, so she was left with no choice but to enter the room and dine alone with Elijah.

He sat at the head of the table wearing a grey suit with snowy white linen, cravat tied impeccably tight at his throat, holding a delicate cup and drinking. He glanced up when he saw her but offered no smile.

'Miss Seymour.' He put his cup down and rose to his feet. 'Do sit down.' He pulled the chair out for her before the hovering servant could do so and she took her seat, a wash of masculine scent overtaking her from his body as he stood close.

Susanna folded her hands on her lap tightly, asking for some eggs and toast when the servant enquired. Elijah regained his seat, leant over, and poured some orange juice. She thanked him, sat with her head bowed as she was served. Elijah looked up, dismissed the servant with a gesture, and the two of them were left alone in the room.

Susanna took a sip of juice. She did not dare lift her eyes.

'Susanna,' Elijah said in an undertone. 'Your mouth is so hot and wicked.'

Her head jerked up. She narrowed her eyes at him, blushing furiously.

He arched a sardonic brow. 'What, I'm not allowed to mention what you did to me last night?'

She gave a fierce shake of her head. 'It was under the influence of wine and you know why I did it. It's not something to be dissected.'

He fixed those crystal blue eyes on her. 'To gain a husband for your sister,' he said.

'Correct,' she said tartly.

'And not because the thought of my cock in your mouth excited you beyond reason?'

Susanna shoved her chair back with indignation.

'Sit down.' His tone was like a whip. Susanna sank fearfully back to her seat, not taking her gaze from him. 'If I want to discuss it, we'll discuss it. Contrary to what you might think, I don't usually have women taking such liberties with me and then preferring it was swept under the carpet.'

She curled her lip. 'Have I bruised your delicate ego, Mr Storm? Perhaps you can't handle a woman taking control.'

She saw the fury on his face and let her chair fly back, running across the room as fast as her gown would allow her. He reached the door before her, slamming it shut, grabbing her arm and pulling her around.

'It's true I prefer the control, but that's not to say I didn't enjoy being mastered by you,' he said, fingers gripping her tight and eyes burning into hers. 'But let's not pretend that was an end to it. It was just the beginning.'

Susanna shook her head, aghast. 'No.'

'Yes.' His arm curled about her waist. He pulled her against his muscular body and she felt the hard beating of his heart. She braced her hands on his chest, turning her face away as he tried to kiss her.

Stumbling from his grip, he merely pressed her back against the door, thrusting a thigh between hers as his lips claimed hers savagely. Susanna gasped. She had had kisses before, some none too chaste, but no one had ever kissed her with such raw passion before.

She tried to fight him but it was pointless. Her body responded to him unbidden. She curved a hand around his neck and he pressed closer, deepening the kiss, tongue slipping between her lips. Susanna let out a low moan. She felt his erection against her hip and her whole body shuddered with emotion. When he let her go, she sagged weakly against the door, shattered, fingers touching her lips unconsciously.

Elijah's desperate expression waned, as though he had mastered the beast within him. He reached out, trailed fingertips over the curve of her cheek tenderly, and she instantly jerked away. Fumbling behind her, she yanked open the door and fled.

Susanna slumped back in the carriage as they set off down the driveway away from the house with Elijah standing at the door watching them go. Lucy was wrapped in her cloak like an invalid, foot elevated on the seat next to Susanna. She chattered endlessly about what a gentleman Mr Storm was while Susanna remained silent.

This was not how it should have gone. She should have been going home with Lucy's hand firmly secured, not with her lips burning and her body still craving Elijah's touch.

Chapter Six

A GLOOM FELL OVER the house like mourning when it was reported that Elijah had gone back to London for the foreseeable future. Lucy kept to her chamber with no attempt made to rehabilitate her ankle with exercise, and Mrs Seymour took to her bed as though someone had died. Susanna guessed it was the smashing of her dreams her mother objected to. She herself steamed with impotent fury. She had compromised herself with that man, had received his promise that he would seek her sister's hand and, instead, he had fled like the philanderer he was.

Summer had turned to early autumn, bright crisp days and fallen leaves, when the thunder of hooves echoed up the drive and a man presented his calling card. Susanna lifted her head from her book as Mrs Seymour flew into the drawing room, hands flapping, generous bosom heaving.

'Mr Storm is come back!'

She was followed by Lucy, who seemed to have made a miraculous recovery. Both women had clearly forgotten their stupor, and were happy for the rake to come back into their lives and make his insincere apologies. Susanna curled her lip. She stood.

'If you'll excuse me, I have a headache.'

But it was too late. Richard arrived at the door, announcing loudly, 'Mr Elijah Storm.'

Elijah strode in. Elizabeth and Lucy almost swooned

simultaneously. He was dressed all in black, not a speck of colour about him anywhere, his hair still indecently short. His pale eyes flickered over Susanna, unreadable.

He bowed low at the three women. 'My deep regret at my sudden departure,' he said, mainly addressing Elizabeth. 'My mother was taken ill.'

Susanna regarded him suspiciously. Was it the truth? She doubted anything this man said.

Elizabeth made a sympathetic clucking sound like a constipated chicken. 'Nothing serious, I hope?'

'She was gravely sick,' Elijah said, 'but is now on the road to recovery. I hope to spend several weeks at my estate but would have to leave again should she take a turn for the worse.'

'Of course,' Elizabeth said.

Lucy didn't speak. She gazed at Elijah in rapture.

There was an uncomfortable silence, during which Elijah cleared his throat. 'Actually, it is Mr Seymour I have come to see.'

Elizabeth turned purple. Her eyes bulged from her head and she clasped her hands at her bosom, barely able to stay upright with excitement. 'Of course. Richard!' She yelled to the butler, who hovered in the hall. 'Please show Mr Storm to my husband's study.'

The butler bowed. Elijah inclined his head politely, threw Susanna a quick glance, and turned on his heel, riding boots tapping on the parquet floor.

Elizabeth fell into a chair in a near faint, fanning herself theatrically with her hand. 'Oh Lucy! This is it!'

Susanna regarded her sourly. There could be no doubt that Elijah had come to ask for Lucy's hand in marriage. But instead of satisfaction that he had finally kept his end of the bargain, she only felt deep, wrenching agony. She sat down, her novel clutched hard to her chest, where the worst of the pain was located. That a man like him could make her feel like this, for the first time in her life ... It seemed incomprehensible. To watch him lost to her sister, a man who had stirred her so passionately. How would she ever recover from this? She looked at Lucy, pale and tense with excitement, pacing the drawing room as though waiting to hear a sentence pronounced and she felt tender. The better woman had won. She should wish Lucy well. While some of Elijah's behaviour and temperament was suspect, her marriage would never be short of passion.

The three of them waited in tense silence. Elizabeth called for water and smelling salts. Lucy hovered by the window, plucking at the curtains with anxious fingers. And Susanna sat perfectly still and wished with all her heart that she had never met Elijah Storm.

It seemed an eternity before a door opened distantly. Two sets of footsteps sounded down the hall. Edward and Elijah appeared in the doorway; Edward beaming, Elijah coolly content. Both of them looked towards Susanna and she flushed at the attention, confused.

Elizabeth gathered her wits and lurched to her feet. 'Mr Seymour?' she addressed her husband. 'You have something to share with us?'

Edward rubbed his hands together. 'Indeed I do. Mr Storm has asked for our daughter's hand in marriage.'

Elizabeth threw her hands up. 'Oh God be praised! I hope you said yes, Edward!'

'Of course, Elizabeth,' Edward said, his tone gently reproving. 'That is if Susanna herself consents, because I would no more give her away against her will than I would ...'

Elizabeth cut him off. 'You mean Lucy?'

Every woman in the room was stiff and silent. Susanna stared dumbly at her father.

'No, my dear, I mean Susanna,' he pronounced.

Susanna's legs would have buckled had she not been sitting down. She felt the blood drain from her face and she looked from Edward to Elijah in increasing panic. This couldn't be true. Why would he do this? What about Lucy and his promise? Her mother would never forgive her for this.

Elizabeth stifled a little cry behind her handkerchief and burst into noisy tears.

'My dear,' Edward said, looking at Mr Storm with some embarrassment.

Meanwhile, Lucy ran from the room in hysterics.

'I don't understand,' Elizabeth sobbed. 'Mr Storm, I presented Lucy to you in the most transparent of gestures. She is our hope of a good match. Susanna, she …' She didn't dare look at her daughter. 'She's a maid now, beyond hope of a husband. You have had your head turned, I understand, but you must realise Lucy is the right woman for you and …'

Elijah interrupted firmly and gently. 'Mrs Seymour, I'm sorry to disappoint you. I have no particular feeling for Lucy and I have always promised I would never marry a woman for money, for the match or any such silly thing evident these days. I ardently love and admire Susanna and I wish your blessing for her hand.'

Susanna stared up at him with her senses swimming. Her ears must be playing tricks. He had not just declared his love, had he? There must be some mistake. This philanderer had teased and tormented her and shown himself to be a man of the loosest morals. Why exactly did he wish her hand, and what made him think she would actually consent to be his wife? For a start, as if she could disregard her sister so cruelly.

Elizabeth swayed in place, shaking her head, still at a

loss to comprehend.

Susanna rose quickly from her seat. 'Thank you for your kind invitation, Mr Storm,' she said with her voice as firm as she could make it. 'I regret I am unable to accept.' She inclined her head and marched past him.

Behind her, she heard Elizabeth give a wail.

Angry voices came from the study as Susanna hovered outside later that day. She had lain on her bed for hours, weeping at the cruel twist of fate that would have Elijah Storm declaring his love for her. From down the hall, she had heard Lucy's racking sobs and was unable to comfort her. Her sister would now see her as the enemy, someone who had stolen the man of her dreams away.

'In God's name, woman, what does it matter which daughter he chooses as long as we have found a husband for one of them?' Edward said in exasperation.

'Edward, Lucy was meant for him. Mr Storm in his contrary fashion, as only he can, has made a mockery of us all, of me, of poor Lucy. Clearly he plays with poor Susanna to amuse himself at our expense.'

Susanna leant against the wall with tears in her eyes and a hand over her mouth.

'That was not the way Mr Storm put his case to me,' her father said. 'He waxed lyrical in his admiration for Susanna. I was left in no doubt as to his feelings.'

Susanna shook her head. She refused to believe that Elijah's feelings extended beyond needs of the flesh. He toyed with her. He would marry her and then he would disappear for weeks on end to card games and houses of ill repute. Oh, she knew his type, no matter her sheltered upbringing. He absolutely could not be allowed to get away with this. She clenched her fists. She would show him. God, she would show him.

* * *

The rain was lashing down in sheets as she descended from the carriage on the driveway of Rainton Grange and was shown inside by the curious butler. Her behaviour was scandalous, of course, for a single woman to turn up uninvited at the home of such a notorious bachelor as Mr Storm. Well, she didn't much care what the gossips would say. She doubted Elijah himself was loose-lipped even if he was loose in every other area.

'Miss Seymour to see Mr Storm,' she said as the butler helped her off with her damp cloak and bonnet and took her gloves. Footsteps sounded on the marble floor and the man of the house appeared.

'Thank you, Reuben,' he said. 'That will be all.'

The butler bowed and withdrew, taking Susanna's outdoor clothes with him.

Elijah looked highly amused, those crystal blue eyes dancing with mirth. 'Why, Miss Seymour, you're all wet. Perhaps I can interest you in getting out of those clothes before you catch a chill?'

Susanna stalked forward. She beat her fists in rage against his chest. 'You beast! Why must you play with me and my family this way? What has poor Lucy done to you that you would disrespect her so?'

Elijah's eyes flashed. He gripped her wrists, hard enough to hurt. 'You think I play with you? You think my feelings for you show disrespect to your sister?'

'Yes!' she cried.

He shook her breathless before releasing her abruptly. 'You fool,' he spat. 'You have no idea.'

She followed his lithe body with an anxious gaze as he paced away, seemingly striving to recover himself. He raked a hand through his hair, leaving it dishevelled, and breathed heavily.

'You don't know how you compromise yourself by coming here,' he said finally, with a cunning glint in his eye. 'The things I could do to you.'

Heat rose to Susanna's cheeks. Her body flooded with warmth and sensation, her nipples tightening, her groin pulsing. His forbidden words raised all kinds of taboo images no lady had any right to be thinking, centred on his mouth, his hands, and that thick, glorious cock just made for pleasure. She ached between her legs for him.

She bit her lip, attempting to stare him down with an angry mask in place, but she was fighting a losing battle. She turned to flee, but it was too late. He caught her around the waist, pulled her against the hard length of his body. She whimpered at the feel of his erection against the small of her back. His breath drifted over her ear. 'Let me,' he whispered. 'Let me.'

He cupped her breasts and she arched shamelessly into his touch despite the layers of clothing separating them. His mouth trailed down her neck, planting heated kisses, raising an inferno of desire.

Quite suddenly, he gripped her hand, swung her around to pull her after him. She gasped as he forced her down at the foot of the stairs and fell to his knees. Lifting her skirts, he pushed her thighs apart.

In both mounting lust and blind panic, she tried to fight him. He buried his head beneath her skirts, strong hands keeping her legs prised open, mouth at the top of one stocking, teasing her burning skin.

She gripped his hair with a cry of outrage as he tore her linen underwear apart in his strong hands, and then his mouth was on her swollen, desperate flesh.

She bucked in Elijah's grip as his tongue flickered over her clitoris, aching and sensitive. He slid his hands under her backside, lifted her to his face, holding her firm, and swiped down her slit, burying between her folds.

Susanna shook and moaned. Elijah teased her up and down one more time before he concentrated that wicked tongue on her hard bud, lapping, lashing and tormenting ferociously, intent, it seemed, on driving her to the fastest, wildest orgasm imaginable.

She lurched and trembled in his grip, unspeakably noisy as he brought her to the edge. He pushed two fingers into her slick warmth and she cried out, knowing she was about to experience a climax unlike anything her own hand could deliver. Senses scattered, she arched desperately against his mouth, wailing as the ecstasy took her, hands clutching his head, holding him in place in case he slid away before she could milk the last waves. But Elijah stayed at his task, tongue frantic as she convulsed, crying out, legs juddering for long seconds that seemed to go on and on and on.

Finally she could take no more of his tongue on her sensitive flesh. She pushed his face away, head dropping back, hands supporting herself on the stairs as she realised the discomfort in her back.

She was sweaty, dishevelled, soaking wet, her hair loose around her face, legs splayed wantonly.

Elijah remained kneeling between her thighs. He wiped the back of his hand over his mouth and smiled, not lewdly, not smugly, but tenderly at her, and her already hammering heart knocked some more.

'Susanna,' he said, 'never have I more enjoyed giving a woman such pleasure in my life.'

Blood flooded her already flushed face. His countenance was ardent and sincere. She couldn't bear him like this, preferring the lecherous Lothario. She slid her torn underwear free and yanked her skirts down. He rose to his feet, the bulge in his breeches massive, and held out his hand, but she shrugged it aside. She tried not to look as he not so discreetly adjusted himself beneath his tight constriction. He stepped aside to allow her passage. His saliva filmed her thighs as she headed for the door with her legs unsteady.

Balling up her drawers, she tossed them back at him. 'Here. A present for you.' She slammed the door behind her and ran coatless through the downpour.

The startled coachman hurried down quickly to help her inside from the thundering rain, and she collapsed against the seat as they raced down the driveway. Susanna trembled violently, eyes closed, reliving every devastating moment of what Elijah had just done to her.

Chapter Seven

HER MOTHER AND SISTER were not speaking to her the next day. Her father called her solemnly into his office and she sat nervously at his desk while the fire in the grate crackled and popped.

'So,' he said. 'Mr Storm.'

She blushed just to hear his name.

'Your colour tells me everything I need to know.'

Susanna twisted her hands in her lap. 'I feel a certain – affinity for the man, father,' she said. 'But not at the expense of my mother or sister's feelings.'

Edward waved his hand impatiently. 'Your mother be damned.'

She gaped at the sedition.

'The man asked for your hand, Susanna. He sat before me and assured me in all honesty, with his hand on his heart, that he would love and cherish you for the rest of his life. And you rejected him summarily!'

She kept her head bowed. 'I don't believe a word he says, father.'

'And why the devil not?'

She couldn't tell him about Elijah's bold, lascivious behaviour. About their intense sexual chemistry that she suspected would fizzle out once she had to wake up next to him every morning and sit opposite him at the breakfast table for the rest of her life.

'I don't think he wants me for the right reasons.'

'He wants you for the right reasons, my girl. You're proud, headstrong, intelligent, and fiercely independent. In short, his perfect match.'

'He said that?'

'In so many words. You'll give him a run for his money. Do you really think your sister could tame a man like him the way you could?'

She stared at him. 'Is that what you think? That I could tame him? That he *wants* me to tame him?'

'Yes.'

She dropped her gaze, fingers plucking nervously at a loose thread on her gown. 'I can't, father.'

'Child, what am I going to do with you?'

She shook her head miserably, and knew the real reason for her reluctance. She was altogether too afraid of the strength of her feelings for Elijah.

The following day was bright enough to venture outside. Susanna bemoaned the loss of her favourite cloak, bonnet, and gloves to Elijah and hoped he wouldn't be foolish enough to attempt to return them. She wandered over the lawns and down into the woods, kicking her way through piles of red and golden leaves, listening to the crackling underfoot, the melodic sound of birdsong overhead. She heard the rushing of the river, swollen from the torrential rain that week, as she stepped into the clearing and realised that, actually, lightning did strike twice.

A midnight black horse stood tethered to an oak. A pile of clothes lay on the bank. In the feisty current, Elijah Storm swam naked.

Susanna stopped dead.

He spotted her instantly. He stood, the water lapping around his bare, muscular chest. 'Miss Seymour, as I live and breathe. I have items of your clothing awaiting you at my home.'

She glowered at him. 'Why are you permanently undressed?'

'I thought you liked me that way? You yourself undressed me one evening as I seem to remember. You tore at my breeches like you were opening a box of chocolates.' He smirked. He walked closer to the bank and she watched the water fall slowly down his rippling torso, revealing a line of dark hair that disappeared down his belly. She swallowed. His biceps were huge, as though he felled trees for a living or indulged in other manual labour. The power of his body awed and disconcerted her.

'An accident,' she said, her voice small.

He raised an eyebrow, stepping closer still so the waterline fell to the dark hair at his groin, and she nearly whimpered. 'See anything you like?' he asked teasingly, standing still.

She shook her head, lips pressed tightly together.

'Then perhaps I should climb out.'

'I don't think so,' she said hastily.

'Why? Worried you won't be able to control yourself?'

She laid a hand on the horse's flank for reassurance. 'The only one of us who exhibits loss of control on a frequent basis is you, Mr Storm.'

He laughed loudly. 'Is that so?'

'Yes.' She lifted her chin. 'If I undressed right now, you would be unable to stop yourself rushing from the water to claim me, am I right?'

He regarded her with his head cocked on one side as though trying to work out if it was a trick. And it was. She would not end up in the same compromised position as last time with him. Instead, if she could turn the tables she would tease him so badly he would finally realise he was never going to get anywhere with her and abandon the chase. A little ache in her chest was easy to dismiss.

'No,' he said stonily. 'If you wished me to stay here and admire you from afar, I could do that.'

'Could you?'

'I could, although I'd rather be over there pinning you to that tree and driving into you.'

Susanna's face flamed. She pictured the image all too well. She put her hands to the fastenings on her bodice and he stared, eyes riveted. She unlaced deftly and pulled the gown down her arms to her waist, standing in her restrictive corset with breasts bulging from the top. Elijah licked his lips. A slight flush rose over his cheeks. The water lapped at his belly, receded; for a moment she saw the head of his cock, tumescent.

He was always so hard for her. The knowledge made her legs shake and her fingers tremble as she unlaced the corset and bared her breasts proudly. Elijah drew in his breath. He ground his teeth.

'God in heaven, woman.' He stumbled to the bank and she reared back, pressing against the tree. Elijah stood there in the shallows with his hard prick dripping water, his heavy balls tight and swaying. It was all she could do not to run and fling herself upon him.

'Stay right there, Mr Storm, or I shall scream,' she informed him.

He gave a little growl. 'Then show me,' he said. 'Show me everything or God help me ...'

Susanna leant back against the tree, breasts thrust out. She cupped them in her hands, squeezing, massaging, and pinching the nipples between her thumb and forefinger until they stood taut like ripe cherries. Elijah's gaze burned her.

'I would taste you,' he declared throatily. 'I would taste every part of you when you are mine.'

'But I will never be yours, Mr Storm,' she shot back. 'This is our swansong. You shall realise there is nothing between us but need.'

A dark shadow fell across his face, his eyes turning icy. 'And need is a fine thing to start a marriage,' he declared. 'As God is my witness, you would not leave my bedchamber for a week.'

Susanna's heart surged and her underwear flooded. 'You wish me as a toy for the bedroom, yes? You have nothing to offer me but a hard prick, Mr Storm!'

A sardonic smile failed to reach his eyes. He curled his hand around the aforementioned prick and started a slow stroking. 'Isn't that just what you need, Miss Seymour? My cock stoking your insides until you scream.'

She tried to tear her gaze from the sensual motion of his hand. His erection glistened with water, a pearly drop rolling from the tip.

'Now show me,' he said. 'Show me how you pleasure yourself when you think of me.'

She bit her lip to hide a furious cry, then scooped up her skirts and thrust a desperate hand down her drawers. His glance fixed on her groin as she started to rub her wet slit frantically, watching his wanking hand all the while.

'Marry my sister,' she said, panting.

'No,' he said. 'Marry me.'

'No.'

'Then I will marry someone else and, one day, I will come back here, and next time I catch you in these woods, you will be mine, Susanna Seymour. No false modesty, no pretence. I will throw you down and I *will* have that carefully preserved maidenhead of yours.'

She blanched. 'You would take me by force, sir?'

He threw his head back and laughed. '*Force*? You little minx.' And suddenly he launched a charge, water showering him as he lurched up the bank, thundering towards her. Susanna shrieked, ran from him with her skirts bunched and her breasts exposed.

Her speed was no match for his. He gripped her arm, pulled her to a halt, and sat down abruptly on a tree stump. Her momentum carried her face down over his lap, where he held her with a cool, heavy hand on the small of her back.

'Let me go!'

He ignored her. 'This is what you deserve, and it's what you shall have.' He raised her skirts, yanked her underwear down.

She wriggled and gasped before he brought his hand down on her bottom in a slap. Susanna cried out.

'Hush.' He spanked her again. 'The more noise you make, the more I shall spank you.'

Susanna bit her hand. She wailed around it as he spanked both cheeks soundly until they glowed. But the position of submission was startlingly pleasurable for her, even though she would never admit it to him. She was wet between her legs and she writhed on his lap with his naked cock pressed into her belly.

He touched her, sliding a finger along her slit, gathering the moisture and circling her bud. She hissed, gripping at handfuls of grass, the blood rushing to her head. Elijah laughed softly. He parted her buttocks with one hand and circled her most intimate area with a wet thumb while his finger continued to torment her clit.

Susanna tried to jerk away in outrage as her entrance fluttered around his touch. He took no notice but continued to rub and press until his thumb penetrated her. She cried out. He pushed two fingers into her hole, and used his other hand to rub her clit. With those talented hands, he rubbed and fingered and fucked her all the way to a screaming climax.

She clenched around his fingers, wave after wave of intense contractions until she fell limply on his lap, almost rolling off before he caught her.

She dimly heard Elijah laugh. 'How many more times do I have to make you come before you marry me?'

She struggled to stand, pulling her drawers up over her ravaged, red backside. 'A hundred,' she said defiantly, stuffing her breasts back into her corset.

Elijah grinned, licking at his fingers. 'A helping hand would not go amiss,' he said, motioning to his straining cock.

'Go to hell. Playtime is over.' Susanna stalked away through the trees, fastening her dress as she went.

Chapter Eight

IN THE WAR AGAINST Elijah Storm, Susanna declared that she had won this round. Although she hadn't intended to be caught by him and spanked soundly, nor driven to an orgasm against her will using her most taboo hole, nonetheless, *she* had climaxed, and *he* hadn't. Just like last time. As far as she was concerned, his balls must be near blue by now. She grinned to herself as she lay on her bed later that day, lingering on the scene in her mind. Nonetheless, she hadn't achieved her intended aim – the withdrawal of his proposal and the transfer of his affections to Lucy. She would have to accept that, sadly, her sister was not going to gain a husband out of this wild man. It was for the best.

What she needed was to get rid of Mr Storm once and for all and empty her heart and body of his presence. She hit upon a plan. She would take Lucy to London to stay with their Aunt Georgina and there woo the most eligible of men.

Her mother offered barely a protest, confined to her room in mourning. They set off a week later, Lucy sullen by her side but coming to accept after long explanations that Susanna had not sought Mr Storm's attentions and did not intend to usurp Lucy in his affections.

By the time they stopped at an inn for supper, Lucy was positively excited about their upcoming visit and the chance to meet so many eligible bachelors. Susanna was less so. The cold knot below her ribs told her she pined for Elijah in the most shameful of ways. This could not go on. She would have to lose herself in merriment and flirting for the duration of their trip.

They arrived next day and Georgina, their mother's sister, greeted them effusively at the door of her townhouse. Never married, she had a certain reputation with Elizabeth – flighty, flirtatious, and fond of dangerous assignations. Susanna suspected Elizabeth's disapproval was based on envy. It seemed to her that Georgina lived the most exciting and free of lives – no one to answer to, no one to please but herself. Why would every woman not want that? Perhaps Susanna could have it too. Maybe her father would be willing to set her up in a small house near to her aunt and she could embark on the same sort of thrilling life as Georgina. But Mr Storm crept into her thoughts again. If he married someone else, it would kill her, she knew.

The first night was a dance at the stunning mansion of an acquaintance of Georgina's. Mr Craig was a silver-haired bachelor in his 50s and was so delighted to see her aunt that Susanna wondered about the true nature of their friendship. Susanna and Lucy danced all night, wooed by a succession of rich, titled men, and Lucy came away breathless, eyes shining, clearly having forgotten all about Mr Storm.

Susanna, however, had not. She compared them all to Elijah and found them wanting. Angrily she argued with her subconscious. What exactly was there to admire about this man? His sardonic nature? His wanton sexuality? Or the way he looked when his erection was deep in her mouth and he trembled on the brink of climax? She shook when she thought about it. A certain kind of vulnerability had been revealed that night. A chink in his armour.

Instead of exploiting it, she had allowed him to take the upper hand once more. But there was no denying she preferred it that way. Being mastered by him.

The next day, Lucy and Georgina both pleaded headaches so Susanna took the carriage into town alone. Too much wine, she knew, and while her own head was delicate, it wasn't enough to keep her to her bed. Plenty of fluids and fresh air would do the trick. She wandered the squalid streets of London, looking in shops, giving coins to beggars and street urchins. She bought her mother and father trinkets although she wasn't sure her mother deserved a present.

As the carriage rumbled along the uneven street, Susanna glanced into an alleyway and was startled by what she saw. A woman who must have been in her 60s trying to fight off two ragamuffins, intent on grabbing her bag and rifling through her pockets.

'Stop!' she cried to the driver, rapping the underside of the carriage with her umbrella. The horses lurched to a halt at his bidding and she jumped down at the mouth of the alley. Making a terrific noise and holding her umbrella like a weapon, she charged into the chaos with more courage than she really felt, her heart hammering. By this time the woman was on her knees and the boys had taken a small, drawstring bag from her. They scampered away at Susanna's approach.

Susanna crouched and looked at the badly shaken woman. Her bonnet was gone and her carefully coiffured grey hair fell loose over her face. She was attractive, but looked unwell, with dark circles under her eyes, her skin tinted a waxy colour.

'Let me help you,' Susanna said, placing a hand under the trembling woman's elbow just as Georgina's carriage driver arrived on the other side.

The woman glanced up, fixing pale blue eyes on her. 'Thank you,' she murmured in a soft expiration.

'We'll take you home,' Susanna said, and the driver lifted the frail woman into his arms and carried her from the alleyway.

The woman dozed, seemingly exhausted, all the way back to a smart Chelsea townhouse. The driver lifted her down from the cushions, and Susanna hurried to the door and rapped.

The liveried butler who answered gaped at them and stood back at once, allowing admission. 'Mistress,' he said, wringing his hands. 'What has happened?'

'She was set upon by some boys,' Susanna explained.

'Shall I go upstairs?' asked the driver.

'Yes,' Susanna directed, 'and fetch the doctor,' she told the butler.

The man scurried off and Susanna ascended behind the driver. He carried her into a woman's bedchamber and laid her down on the bed. A fire burned cheerily in the grate as Susanna bent and removed the woman's shoes before pulling up the quilt from the foot of the bed, covering her to her neck.

The woman blinked sleepily at her, reached for Susanna's hand. 'Thank you to you both.'

Susanna pulled up a chair. She held the woman's hand and stroked it with her other while the driver hovered by the fire.

'Do you want to leave me here?' she asked. 'I'll wait until the doctor comes and send a note for you to bring me back.'

He inclined his head. 'Very well, miss.'

When he had gone, the room was silent save for the crackling of logs in the hearth and the soft, sighing breath of the woman in the bed. Susanna sat content to hold her hand as the woman slipped into slumber. As her eyes grew heavy in the soporific heat, a commotion downstairs roused her, voices raised before thundering boots sounded on the stairs.

Susanna braced herself for the anxiety and upset of a concerned relative as the door burst open. She almost reeled back in her chair when confronted with Elijah Storm.

He saw her instantly, his face turning from grief and worry to startled surprise. Then his attention switched rapidly to the woman in the bed, and Susanna hurriedly pushed her chair back as he stalked around the foot of the four-poster.

'Mother,' he said, reaching for the woman's hand, and Susanna wondered then why she hadn't seen it before. The woman's attractive face carried more than a hint of her son's beauty.

'It's all right, Elijah,' Mrs Storm murmured softly. 'I have been in good hands.'

Elijah turned his crystal blue gaze on Susanna and she blushed, hands twisted together, awed by him as she usually was.

A sharp knock sounded at the door, and Elijah called admittance. He strode quickly to greet the small, efficient looking man with the medical bag. 'Doctor Tully, thank you for coming.'

The doctor nodded, approaching the patient. 'Mrs Storm,' he said, and the patient reached out for his hand with a tired smile, obviously on good terms with the man.

Elijah gestured to Susanna and she hurried to the door with him behind her. He closed the door and instantly had her hemmed in against the wall.

'Miss Seymour,' he said, his eyes large with sorrow and ardour. 'I have no words to express my gratitude.'

She lifted a hand, attempting to wave away his thanks with embarrassment. He came closer, looking down at her intently beneath the rim of her bonnet. 'My mother has been unwell, as you know, and a shock such as today could set back her recovery significantly. If you hadn't acted so quickly …'

'I was merely in the right place,' she said, stifling a sigh as Elijah cupped the back of her neck with gentle fingers.

'It was more than that,' he said, staring deeply into her eyes, his voice a low, warm caress. 'You are a woman of courage and fire. You care enough to help a stranger on the street regardless of your own peril.' He paused, took a deep breath. 'You are the woman I want by my side. To make me complete.'

Susanna swallowed, her palms damp, her eyes abruptly dewing. 'Mr Storm,' she said, but the words deserted her because she didn't know what she wanted to say.

Elijah lowered his head. His lips brushed hers like the kiss of a butterfly's wings before he drew back. Clearing his throat, he said, 'My driver will take you home.'

Her legs trembling, Susanna moved to the head of the stairs. Elijah stepped up behind her, touching her waist with fleeting fingers. 'I hope to see you again while you are in London,' he said against her ear.

Susanna didn't reply. She descended the steps and was greeted again by the butler, who offered her refreshments. She refused and asked to be taken home. As he showed her out to the carriage, she looked up and saw Elijah at the top of the stairs, watching her.

When she got home, Susanna was in a state of nervous excitement. Making sure Lucy was out of the way, she confessed about Elijah to her aunt and what had happened with his mother that afternoon. Georgina sat watching her with gleaming eyes like a cat, and admitted that Elizabeth had sent a letter with Lucy describing the Seymours' scandalous new neighbour and how he had broken Lucy's heart in favour of Susanna.

'She had nothing nice to say about Mr Storm other than a comment on the size of his purse,' she said, lifting a handkerchief to her face to hide a smirk.

Susanna felt herself blush a little. 'Mr Storm has many fine attributes,' she said.

'Does he really?' Georgina pulled her chair closer. 'Do tell all.'

'Aunt, really.'

'Oh stuff,' Georgina said airily. 'Are we not both women of the world? The way you talk about this Mr Storm tells me you have been intimate with him in some fashion.'

Susanna stared. 'Aunt, you mustn't tell my mother.'

Georgina snorted. 'I thought you knew me better than that, Susanna. Am I not to be your confidante and your advisor when it comes to the tricky subject of men?'

Susanna glanced around as though the walls had ears. 'Well, aunt, the second time I saw him, I caught him engaged in the most intimate behaviour on our land …'

Chapter Nine

THE SISTERS' STAY IN London continued in a whirlwind of parties courtesy of their aunt, but Susanna was maudlin. She couldn't forget the intensity in Elijah's eyes when he had said those words about her making him complete. She swung between swearing him off for good and running to his side to take back her refusal of his proposal. She suspected it still stood, that he waited for her to change her mind, but just how long would he wait before his head was turned and another woman claimed him? Men like Elijah Storm came along once in a lifetime, Susanna was sure of that.

The final party of their stay was at a mansion in the Surrey countryside that belonged to an old friend of Georgina's. The three women were ensconced in rooms for the evening on their arrival and, on their descent, were greeted by Lady Yvette Mario and her husband, Thomas. Georgina had murmured something salacious about her relationship with Yvette and Thomas in the carriage on the way there and Susanna wondered if she had misheard.

The house bustled with finely dressed guests, ladies dripping in jewels and men in their smartest frock coats and cravats. Waiters in livery moved smoothly between the bodies with trays of champagne and canapés. Lucy gaped around her with wide eyes while Susanna was more subtle, demurely watching men from beneath her lashes. She wore a new gown of white silk with a broad black sash and intricate corsetry at the back. Lucy was radiant in sapphire blue.

The three women chatted with some of Georgina's friends before moving into the grand ballroom and taking a table near the floor. Georgina tossed back champagne like it was going out of style and Susanna felt a little tipsy too, despite trying to keep her self-control. Lucy chattered excitedly about a man in uniform watching her and then she gave a gasp, put her hand over her mouth. Susanna followed her gaze.

Standing with a blond-haired man against the wall, wearing black and white evening attire, was Elijah Storm. Susanna's heart leapt and thudded wildly against her ribs as Elijah spotted her and leant close to his companion's ear to say something above the music.

'That blackguard,' Lucy said darkly as Elijah pushed himself lazily off the wall and strolled around the edge of the dance floor like a nonchalant cat stalking its prey.

'Hush, Lucy,' Susanna scolded. 'There is no need for rudeness.'

'Just because Mr Storm has you by your heart, or indeed other parts, is no reason for me to like him,' Lucy replied snottily.

Susanna kicked her hard under the table. Lucy gave a little cry and sank miserably into her chair.

Elijah reached the table. He regarded the three ladies with blue eyes dazzlingly bright. 'Miss Seymour and Miss Seymour.' He bowed low.

'Mr Storm,' Susanna said with a coolness she didn't feel. 'If I may present my Aunt Georgina.'

Georgina held out a hand eagerly, all heaving bosom and fluttering lashes, and Elijah smiled and took it, barely sweeping her knuckles with his lips. 'Charmed.'

There was an uncomfortable silence as Elijah stood

looking at Susanna like there was no one else in the room.

'Mr Storm,' Georgina piped up. 'Why don't you put us all out of our misery and ask Susanna to dance?'

Elijah gave a rueful, almost shy grin. 'Miss Seymour.' He held his hand out. 'May I have this dance?'

Susanna rose to her feet, gathering her skirts. 'You may, Mr Storm.'

His large hand closed around hers, palm warm and intimate. He led her to the dance floor on quaking legs while she asked herself if this had been the best idea.

Elijah wrapped a firm arm around her waist and pulled her close to his hard body. He swept her expertly around the floor to a fast waltz.

'How is your mother?' Susanna asked nervously.

'Much recovered, thank you,' he replied, looking down into her eyes from his lofty height. 'I'm not sure I expressed my gratitude adequately enough last time …'

Susanna regarded him questioningly. Was he serious? She remembered the ardent, eloquent thanks and praise he had bestowed on her. She searched his stunning eyes and found both tenderness and passion. She shook her head.

'I'm *persona non grata* with your family now,' he observed.

Thrown by the sudden change of subject, she fumbled for words. 'It has been a difficult time. Lucy has accepted your lack of interest and moved on. As for my mother –' Susanna sighed. 'Time will heal her troubles.'

'She would no more have me in the family now than Lucifer himself,' Elijah suggested.

'And you once suggested you'd rather wed a plump-bottomed stable hand rather than marry into my family,' Susanna said smartly.

Elijah grinned, his pearly teeth blinding. 'Surely it's a man's prerogative to change his mind?'

'No, it's a woman's.'

Elijah dipped her low and almost dropped her, pulling her upright with the blood rushing to her head. She clung to his neck, glaring.

He smiled again. He lowered his voice to a seductive murmur with his lips pressed right against her ear. 'Having already proved yourself my match, I am hoping you will now admit that *I* am *your* match, sweet Susanna.'

She stared up into his mesmerising eyes with her skin tingling all over and her body ablaze with passion for him. She swallowed, afraid of the words that wanted to spill out. And then the dance ended and he strode off the dance floor, tugging her after him. Mindless of the people who saw them go, he led her out onto a misty, cold balcony, and there descended steps into the dark garden.

Susanna hurried to keep up with the strides from his long legs. When she shivered, he stripped off his frock coat hurriedly and wrapped it around her shoulders. He steered her into a maze of trees, pressing her up against the massive trunk of a beech.

'Susanna,' he said softly, cupping her cheek. 'You're going to drive me out of my mind with desire.'

She trembled, lifting her chin with determination, aware of the silent solitude of the garden. Would she really be able to stop any nefarious plans on his part and, more to the point, did she want to? 'As I've probably already said, Mr Storm, you think with your prick.'

His expression darkened. He pressed her closer against the rough bark, his hard cock jutting into her hip. 'Nay,' he said. 'When it comes to you, I think with both my prick and my heart. The two are entangled. I want you in all ways. Not just the bedroom.' In the darkness, the fire in his eyes was subdued, but she knew it was there.

She licked her lips nervously and immediately he

swooped in, devouring her, his mouth soft and seeking. She opened her lips with a sigh, found his tongue and they stood lip-locked against the tree, his body sinking into hers, moulding her curves to his. She slid her arms around his neck. He scooped her closer, lifting her under her backside, grinding against her, and she gasped, gown constricting her desperately when she wanted nothing more than to be bared to him. His hand found her breast, squeezed through her corset, her nipple standing stiff before it was touched.

He drew back suddenly, letting her slide down the tree. Before she could react, Elijah had slipped to one knee and was fumbling in the pocket of the frock coat that lay discarded on the ground.

'Susanna, I beseech you,' he said as he opened a small box to reveal a ring which sparked like fire under the pale moonlight.

Susanna's jaw dropped. She looked from the ring, to his eyes, and back again. 'Elijah,' she said softly and she saw by his triumphant look that he knew her answer before she did.

He took her hand in a palm that was damp and unsteady, and slipped the ring onto her finger. 'Marry me,' he said urgently.

She touched the soft contour of his cheek and was suddenly sure. 'Yes,' she said.

Elijah rose swiftly to his feet. He lifted her, laughing, off the ground and into his arms and held her close, face pressed into her cleavage.

Chapter Ten

THE WEDDING WAS THE event of the year. People came from all over the country to Elijah's country mansion. Edward walked his elder daughter proudly down the aisle, while Elizabeth sat on the front row of guests looking like she was sucking lemons, Lucy sobbing softly by her side. Elijah's mother, although frail, looked much recovered and sat smiling on the opposite side.

At the top of the room stood Elijah, a formal morning suit hugging his delicious body, his black hair gleaming. He turned around as Susanna approached and his rather nervous expression dissolved into rapture. He lifted her veil before he took her hand.

They stood before the priest and declared their love and exchanged rings; afterwards, Susanna couldn't remember anything apart from the beautiful glow of his crystal eyes. They laughed, danced, and drank. Elijah kept her by his side and introduced her to dozens of people whose names she instantly forgot. Everything seemed surreal. All her belongings had been moved to his home the night before, and in two days they would embark on their honeymoon in France.

She could only think of one thing – their wedding night. She couldn't wait to be alone with him, and his burning gaze when he looked upon her told her he felt the same.

People started to fade away. Susanna was exhausted.

Lucy came up and kissed and hugged her and shyly offered her hand to Elijah, who ignored it and kissed her cheek. Edward shook his hand manfully and welcomed him to the family. Which just left Elizabeth, who hung back unsurely.

'Mrs Seymour,' Elijah said respectfully. 'I will spend the rest of my life making your daughter happy.'

Elizabeth regarded him a moment and then nodded slowly, as though only just realising that was what really counted. A slight expression of shame crossed her face before she stepped forward and presented her hand imperiously to her son-in-law.

Elijah kissed her knuckles. He bade his new family farewell, and the two tearful women and Edward left. Susanna stood watching their carriage disappear down the drive with her husband's arm wrapped around her. They turned, and Elijah closed and bolted the door.

The butler hovered behind them, no doubt waiting for dismissal. 'That will be all, Reuben,' Elijah said. 'Thank you to you all for your hard work today and the days of preparation beforehand.'

The butler bowed. 'May I say what an extraordinary success it was, Mr Storm, and how delightful your bride looked.'

Elijah smiled. 'You may. Thank you. Good night.'

'Good night, sir.' The butler retreated across the huge marble hall towards the kitchen and Elijah pulled Susanna against his broad chest.

'Now, what am I to do with you, Mrs Storm?'

Susanna grinned cheekily to hide her nerves. 'Give me what you've been promising me for months? Something about servicing my three holes, I seem to recall.'

A slow smile spread across his face. 'What a good memory you have, my love.' He swung her up into his arms, and then he carried her up the grand staircase at his leisure, looking into her eyes all the way.

Susanna clung to his neck, trembling with excitement and anticipation that this moment had finally arrived. Elijah carried her into his bedchamber and closed the door firmly behind him before he let Susanna slide slowly down the hard length of his muscular body. She looked around, taking in the sumptuous décor and hangings on the four-poster perfunctorily. She would have done this outside in the barn had he wished, such was her need.

Elijah placed his hands on her shoulders. He drew her close and kissed her, and she melted into him as always. He spun her around. 'Allow me,' he said, and began plucking at the complicated fastenings to her dress with eager fingers.

Susanna shuddered, underwear wet, groin throbbing. He pulled her wedding dress apart and down her arms, and the satin and lace slid into a silky pool around her ankles. She lifted her feet to discard it and Elijah caressed each of her toned calves with one hand as he lifted the dress. He laid out the gown on the back of an ornate chair, then came back, beginning work on her corset, loosening the laces so, finally, for the first time today, she could properly breathe.

As if he could read her mind, he said, 'You may breathe now, my love.'

Susanna giggled, and he slid the corset off her and left her in her thin shift. She turned to face him. He placed his hands on the hem of the shift and stripped it slowly off over her head. She stood bared to him, breasts taut and nipples hard as his gaze perused her.

'I can hardly believe I have permission to touch,' he said in a murmur. 'I'm the luckiest man in the world.'

Boldly, Susanna grasped his hands and put them on her

breasts. Elijah cupped them, squeezing her nipples, and she arched against him with a soft moan.

He wrapped an arm around her waist, pulled her close and bent his head, tonguing and sucking at her nipples. Susanna grasped handfuls of his silky hair. She pushed herself against his mouth, a trail of fire leading down to her groin, and his hand followed the path, cupping her through her silk drawers, finding the fabric wet with her need.

Elijah straightened up. He peeled down her underwear and she kicked it aside, standing in only her stockings and shoes.

'Would you think me terribly depraved if I ask you to leave those both on?' he questioned, a twinkle in his eye.

'That's the least depraved thing I've heard you say yet,' she rejoined with a smile.

Elijah laughed. He lowered his face to her neck and swept heated kisses over her throat. Meanwhile, his hand passed over the hair between her thighs and one finger slipped between her slick lips.

Susanna stifled a cry. His finger penetrated her, fucked her for some seconds until she was dripping, and then he spread her cream over her aching clit, rubbing slowly.

She grasped his wrist, urging him to go faster, rocking against his hand and he looked down, watching, his lashes a sooty sweep against his pale cheeks. 'I hope you know,' he said against her ear, 'that the chances of me lasting tonight once I'm inside you are minimal.'

'As long as you satisfy me, why would I care?' she replied, a touch breathlessly.

'Oh, I'll satisfy you,' he said, now with two fingers in her and his thumb on her clit. 'You'll never need to worry about that, my love. People will see you out and about with such a glow to your cheeks that you will be the talk of the town – a woman whose husband makes her come at least once a day.'

Susanna blushed. She had no doubt any more that Elijah was a man of his word, and shivered to think of all the ways he would please her. 'You're incorrigible,' she said as he withdrew his fingers and led her to the bed.

'I know.' Elijah pushed her down. Then her new husband performed the sauciest, sexiest striptease she had ever seen. He unfastened his cravat and tossed it away. He shrugged his frock coat off his shoulders. His waistcoat dropped to the ground and he kicked his boots off. His rippling torso came into view as he discarded his shirt and stood tall and magnificent. As Susanna watched with awe, Elijah peeled his pants apart and dragged them down his legs.

He'd bothered to wear underwear for his wedding but it was a curious style she had never seen before. Tight, silk shorts that moulded to every curve of his tumescent cock and heavy balls, cupping his assets perfectly. He gripped himself, touching greedily with a sly smile thrown her way, rubbing the head of his cock with his thumb so a wet spot bloomed on the flimsy material.

Susanna bit her lip, gaze riveted on his crotch. 'You always were, and shall remain, the most dreadful tease, my husband,' she said.

Elijah straddled her hips. He plucked the shorts away from his groin so his rampant cock and dark hair reared over the top. 'Dreadful, yes,' he replied. 'Tease, no. I always deliver. Don't ever forget that.'

Susanna reached out. She ran fingers down the length of his rigid shaft through the silk of his underwear and he groaned at her touch. She grasped his thighs, motioning to him. Elijah slid up her body. With legs imprisoning her head, he fed her his cock and she took it gamely, sucking his hot length deep into her throat.

Elijah bucked and hissed. He gripped the bed rail, thrusting lightly, and Susanna grabbed his hard buttocks, lashing his prick furiously.

Elijah's chest heaved. He let out overt moans and, suddenly, he drew back, panting, his eyes heavy and his cheeks flushed. 'Woman, you'll drive me out of my mind before you've finished,' he said. He crawled off her and discarded his underwear. Then he nudged her thighs apart, settling between them.

He touched her again, stroking her clit until it was bullet hard, dipping his fingers into her moist heat and making her crave to be filled. He slid down her body and kissed her mound, tongue flickering over her clit and along her slit in long licks, never lingering because he clearly sensed how close to the edge she was. But Susanna gripped his hair anyway, lifting her desperate sex to his face, gasping for more.

Elijah lifted his head and wiped a hand over the back of his mouth. 'Patience,' he said with a smirk.

'I have no patience when it comes to you, damnable man,' she said. 'Take me and take me now.'

Elijah's eyes went dark. He pinned her to the bed, arms over her head, and she felt steel pressing against her entrance, stretching her. Susanna cried out. He released a wrist, and then held them both in one hand. When she struggled half-heartedly against him, he restrained her further, and it excited her no end. He reached down, grabbed his shaft, and guided it to her.

She panted and arched, groaning as he slid the head through her wetness a few times, lubricating himself before he pressed inside. She lifted her legs, clutched him hard with her thighs as he penetrated her, and she nearly screamed with the pain-pleasure of it.

Elijah caught his breath as he sank slowly inside, inch by inch. He rocked forward, sheathing himself deep, and Susanna whimpered, full and aching and, finally, as close as she could get to her husband. He let her go then and she gripped his back, nails digging in as he withdrew slowly and eased back in.

Elijah set a slow, firm pace. He judged her reactions perfectly and watched how he peeled her apart. Soon she was crying for more and he was driving her into the mattress with hard strokes while she clawed at him and wound herself around his hard body.

Her husband sank his teeth lightly into her throat. He tongued the bruise he had left and the heat of his lips and the wetness of his saliva made her burn. She grabbed his head, forcing a kiss on his lips.

'I love you,' she said.

Elijah growled. He gripped her, rolling over and pulling her astride his hips, and she sat up, grinding down, riding him wantonly until his eyes nearly rolled back into his head with pleasure.

He probed between her legs, rubbing her clit furiously with one finger as she bucked and trembled above him, hands braced on his chest and nails scratching. Using his other hand, he squeezed her breast, plucking at her nipple until she arched into his touch, her hand over his.

'And I you,' he said, ardently, his crystal eyes shining. 'My sweet Susanna.'

Susanna's head fell back. He steadied her on his lap as she plunged over the edge into climax and held her firm as she shook with ecstasy through waves and waves.

As she came back to some semblance of sense, numb and deliciously tingly all over, Elijah arched beneath her and released, hips bucking unsteadily, filling her with his copious seed.

Susanna eased off him. She fell onto her back and Elijah lay panting by her side, soft groans spilling from his lips. He turned his head to regard her with sea-blue eyes, a tired, satiated smile playing around his mouth.

'I have no words,' he said, 'other than please tell me when you are recovered and ready to go again.'

Susanna giggled and slapped him on the shoulder as he tumbled onto her. 'I may have promised to honour and obey, but when did I agree to become your concubine?'

'You don't remember?' Elijah asked with a mock-serious face.

Susanna pulled him close. They kissed, slow and long, and Susanna wondered why it had taken her so long to realise this man was her match.

Freefalling
by Zara Stoneley

Chapter One

THE WARMTH OF HIS hand spiralled through her body, sending a buzz of expectancy to every nerve ending as she held her breath, not daring to move, not daring to murmur; just letting the sensual strokes from hip to knee stir the want deep inside her.

Hayley Tring loved this moment between sleep and wakefulness, when the dream was real, when she could feel it, savour it, her whole body floating effortlessly along poised on the edge of orgasm. When sensuality took over from the harsh reality of urgency and want, and time seemed to be suspended.

A sigh escaped her body and she shifted her hips slightly, anticipating the heat of his hand drifting up between her thighs, of his knowing fingers …

'Hey, sleeping beauty, I knew you'd wake eventually.'

Shit. Every iota of dreamy want shot straight from her body as she went from slumber to wide awake. That "eyes-wide-open" kind of wide awake. And all she could see was a broad chest with a sprinkle of damp, curly hairs. A broad chest that smelled of male, of sweat, of sex; a broad chest that she was close enough to taste. All she had to do was open her mouth, reach out with the tip of her tongue …

Or there again maybe not, because it wasn't a wonderful dream – every mind-blowing memory of last night flooded back with crystal clarity. It was reality, going under the name of Tom.

Hayley groaned inwardly. Tom, maybe not the most gorgeous man she had ever set eyes on, but definitely a man she hadn't been able to take her eyes off. A man she had undressed with her mind a million times before he'd introduced himself, which was probably why her brain had assigned him dream status. She knew what moth to the flame meant now. And it was the wrong time to get burnt, so completely and utterly the wrong time. Which was why he shouldn't be here now, however knee-tremblingly gorgeous he was. Why she should have said no. And why, once she worked out how to speak again, she had to tell him to go.

Oh God. She froze a bit more, if that was possible. It wasn't just that she had her hand on him, she was practically hanging on. And her leg was wrapped round his long, hard thigh in a loving death grip. Shit. And what made him 100 per cent, no room for doubt, flesh and blood real was the twitching erection that seemed to be growing by the second, nudging against her crotch. Which could be partly because she'd been rubbing against him like some sex-starved nympho when she'd thought he was her imaginary friend from the land of nod. And could be partly, oh hell, because of the way she'd begged him for more last night. When she'd let excitement and need take over from common sense. Please, if there's a God, let the ground open up and swallow me whole.

Shit. She wanted to move, and not in a seductive way, but how the hell did she do that without disturbing him, without making it all even more real? And awkward.

His chuckle reverberated through her. 'Something we

did must have worn you out.' She could feel the gentle tug, a tug of tingling awareness that was running over her scalp, trickling through her body as he twirled a lock of her hair round his finger. The heat of his other hand on her hip completed the glowing circle of need he was creating in her body. 'How about I make us a nice fry-up, Miss Sexy?'

'No.' She hadn't meant to shout, it just came out. But at least she'd remembered how to speak. She ran her tongue over suddenly dry lips.

'No? You don't do fry-ups?'

'No. I mean, yes, I mean, I do fry-ups but I've got work to do. Lots of work.' Which was almost true. 'Sorry.' Trying to wriggle away didn't seem like a good idea; maybe a quick leap was the answer before her body decided it had its own agenda and her best intentions leapt out of the window. Again.

'Jug of coffee, then?'

'No.' Yes. Boy, she could kill for a good, strong shot of uncomplicated caffeine; it might even straighten her befuddled brain out and answer a few questions. Like why she had a man in her bed the day after she'd sworn to herself she was a male-free zone until she'd got her current commissions finished. Until she knew she could trust herself not to wreck her one big chance.

'That's a shame.' The deep, sure voice hit a spot deep inside her, and partly answered the question; it was a chocolate-coated promise of satisfaction. Warm, melting, smooth ... For heaven's sake, Hayley, get a grip, girl.

'Because it was fun.' His finger traced a lazy circle round her nipple. *Nooo.* A new ripple of awareness spread out across her breast and started to shimmy its way down her stomach. Maybe if she crossed her legs she could stop it going any further. If it wasn't already too late.

'It was lots of fun.' The warmth of his breath ruffled into her hair, sending another wave of something nice, a double assault. But she'd promised herself. Not now, not right now, she really, really mustn't let herself. One night-stand, fine; well, almost fine, apart from the fact that she didn't do one-night stands and didn't know what was supposed to come next. But whatever it was, it didn't include a fry-up, she was fairly sure about that.

Cosy shared breakfast just had to be wrong, had to be asking for trouble. To be avoided. At all costs. Because she just knew the way she'd reacted to him last night meant that it would be far too easy to want more. Or he wouldn't be in her bed now, looking like he belonged there and intended to stay for a repeat performance.

She bit down hard on her bottom lip as he rolled her onto her back and the warmth spread between her thighs. No, no, no. A wave of heat shimmied up her inner body as his palm moved from her knee, stroking its way effortlessly higher, and she was dimly aware of her legs parting wider. She could say no, she should say no. She should scream stop.

His fingers fluttered over her swollen labia and her whole body seemed to sigh and open up that bit wider. She couldn't help it; she just didn't want to say stop. A firm finger slid smoothly into her damp pussy, sending an urgent zing to her brain. A zing that had everything to do with parting her thighs further and absolutely nothing at all to do with being sensible.

'We shouldn't.'

'Shh. You are just so incredibly gorgeous, you know.' His thumb flicked over her hardening nipple. She had to get out of this, but she couldn't move and she didn't want to. His other thumb drifted lazily over her clit and strong, broad fingers dipped deeper into her slick channel.

She moaned; she knew it had to be her who was making that low sound, and he shifted, moving his arm out from under her, propping himself up so that he could look down, his fingers never leaving her.

It was a cruel dream. Tawny eyes, flecked with gold, were looking at her like she was the centre of the universe; an intense look that sent a new wave of juices between her thighs. And he was curling his fingers, rubbing her G-spot with the type of pressure that was just about to make her forget who she was.

He dipped his head, gold eyes still watching her as his tongue snaked a hot path round her breast. His lips took her nipple and slowly drew her into his mouth in a way that sent a flash of flame straight to her pussy.

Oh boy, that was hitting the spot. 'Oh God, please don't stop.'

'Don't worry, I don't intend to, but I can't talk with my mouth full.' A wicked smile flooded his face and then he sucked her slowly back in as his tongue flicked over her sensitised flesh. His eyes darkened as he sucked harder until the pleasure bordered on pain and her clit started to throb. She gasped, and he knew. His thumb rolled over her swollen nub again, and she automatically tipped her pelvis, circling to follow the motion of his hand, to intensify the pressure until it hit a point where she was sure she couldn't bear any more.

'I didn't think men could multi-task.' Christ, that was good.

'Only when it matters.' His warm tongue traced a path from her breast down her stomach, dipped into her navel. He was sucking and teasing at the soft flesh of her stomach, creating a whole new wave of sensation, and she clutched at his hair, winding her fingers in deep as the play of his tongue and lips seemed to blend in with the fingers that were strumming deep inside her pussy. She shut her eyes.

"Open your eyes, Hayley, I want to see you come, but don't you dare come yet.'

It was the last bit that made her tighten, the rough-edged command. How the hell did that work? She'd spent all her life willing her orgasms closer and now he was telling her not to. Which was what did it. That and the sudden pinch of his finger and thumb on her swollen clit, and the glow of lust in his come-to-bed eyes that seemed to know her better than they should.

She was coming, pulsing round his fingers with a force that was rocking right through her body, and all she could do was press down harder against him, open her thighs even wider so that she could feel him deeper.

'Naughty girl.' His fingers curled inside her, sending a fresh ripple through her body. 'I'm going to have to punish you for that.' He slid further down the bed and his mouth was on her, sucking hard on a clit that was close to burning up.

'No, no, Tom.' It was pain, it was agony, it was bliss. She dug her nails into his shoulders and he roughly pulled her tighter against his face, fingers hard against her hips as he lapped at her swollen slit. She couldn't have moved if she wanted to, except she didn't want to. She wanted to moan, to scream, to beg. He lifted her hips, his fingers digging into her bum as his tongue probed deeper, his teeth teasing her swollen nub, and she didn't know if her orgasm had finished and she was coming again or it had never really ended.

He seemed to have all of her in his mouth, his tongue deep, his teeth closing over her mound as he sucked. She bucked against him, shaking in his strong grip as he held her firm, sucking and licking, never stopping until every last tremble has been drawn out of her and she lay in a panting mess.

Then he blew a raspberry on her trembling stomach. 'Shower time, gorgeous.'

Shit. So much for being sensible.

'I can't.' The too-hot coffee scalded her mouth and set her eyes watering.

'You can't?' He tipped his head to one side, narrowing the tiger eyes. 'Or you don't want to?'

'I can't.' Why wasn't she the type of girl who could just say no? It was fun but "bye" would have done just fine. 'I'm sorry, I don't usually … I mean I don't normally … Just …'

'Throw a man out?'

Fuck, he was making this difficult. 'Sleep with someone like that.' He was making her feel so bad. 'Rush into things.'

'Oh, so it's the rushing that bothers you?'

Oh, it wasn't the rushing; it was the needing that bothered her. 'I can't see you again. I promised.' The needing, and the memory of the tears on her face as he'd made her come last night, the gentleness as he'd kissed them away and then wrapped her in his arms.

'You promised? He gave a short, barking laugh. 'I'm suggesting dinner, Hayley, not a Vegas wedding.'

'I promised.'

'How can you promise someone you won't see me again when you didn't know this would happen?' He waved a hand in the direction of the bedroom and heat rushed to her face. 'Unless I'm part of some well-choreographed act?'

'Good God, no. You don't really think I planned all this and …'

'Not really, no. Well, I'd hope I'm not that much of a pushover.' The gruff laugh made her feel guilty.

'I didn't mean you specifically.'

'Oh great, you're telling me I'm one of many now.'

'Shut up, you know I didn't mean that.' He didn't, he couldn't.

'Do I?'

He did. She was making herself sound like some slut. This wasn't going well, worse than she thought it would. 'What I'm trying to say is …' What was she trying to say, exactly? 'I didn't promise I wouldn't see you again, I meant anyone. Men.'

'Men? What is this, some kind of weird vow of chastity in reverse where you can actually have sex, but not date?'

'Don't be stupid.'

'I don't think I'm the one who's being a bit strange here.'

She scowled at him, which just made him give her an even weirder look. 'Look, I'm sorry, last night shouldn't have happened.'

'But it did. And can you honestly say you didn't enjoy it?'

She'd ignore that. 'I promised myself I wouldn't get involved with anyone – I can't, not just now. My work has to be the important thing, I paint and …'

'I know you paint.'

She coloured what she reckoned must be an even deeper shade of embarrassment judging from the way she was burning up. Of course he knew. He'd been at the exhibition last night, which was where they'd met. She closed her eyes. Being invited to show at the prestigious gallery had been a dream come true and it had got even better. The paintings had been selling, the red stickers sending a thrill through her that felt as good as sex. That made her want sex. Her whole body had been buzzing on some adrenalin high with no way down. Then Mark had whispered in her ear that she had a commission, a big commission, a benefactor whose sponsorship could set her up for life. Which made her want to squeal. And the bubbles from just one glass of champagne had ricocheted through her blood straight to her clit. A clit that had gone into overdrive when she'd been introduced to him.

Mark had wisely given her a moment to get over the squealing, bouncing madness before he'd introduced her to the man who had just set her one step closer to success, the beaming Simon who had been knowledgeable, fun and flirty. And then there had been Tom, Tom his associate, Tom who had eyes that seemed to explore her mind and who had gently curved lips that she wanted to feel exploring her body.

She'd been on her way to the ladies', not quite sure if she had the nerve to shut herself in a cubicle and relieve the pressure, when she'd bumped into him again. Literally. A solid wall of muscle clad in designer jeans and open-necked shirt. And she'd kissed him, because he was gorgeous, and because she was horny, and excited, and hot, and buzzing. Which would have been fine if he hadn't taken control and kissed her right back.

He'd pushed her back against the cold, hard wall, trapped her with the heat of his body, and the contrast of hot and cold had heightened every rampant need in her. The moment he ran his tongue along her lips she'd opened her mouth, desperate to taste him, desperate to feel the strength of his tongue inside her.

She swallowed and opened her eyes. He was studying her still. Crap. 'Of course you know.'

He'd rubbed his hand over her breast as he'd kissed

her and the heat had gone straight through her clothes, seeped through her skin and into her bloodstream. She'd rubbed her hips against him, his hard cock nestled between them, rubbing against her slit as though it was meant to be there. "I bet you fuck just like you paint." He'd said that just as she'd wrapped her leg around his waist, just before he'd slipped his hand up between her hot thighs. "Hot, passionate, alive." And he'd whispered that against her neck as his fingered the damp lace crotch of her panties. "Free." He'd said that just as his fingers had slipped inside her, and she'd thrown her head back and come, hard, the orgasm ripping through her, leaving her panting and desperate for more. So she'd grabbed hold of his shirt and tugged him close for another kiss.

Even though he'd hit the nail on the head when he'd said that. Free. She needed to be free. Or she might as well just give up now, and give up on all the hopes and dreams that rolled around the mysterious benefactor he'd been with. The one who could change her life.

'I paint and ...' She looked straight into the tawny eyes; they were steady, warm, flecked with a feline energy she would have liked to see bubble to the surface, ignite, spread in a molten pool around her. 'That new commission I got with your friend last night is important to me.' Really important, I can't let anyone distract me this time, not again. She was almost whispering, almost sorry, which was stupid. And she was dying to reach out and finger the front of his shirt. Which was even more stupid.

'I'm sure it is.' His warm hands came down and rested gently on her shoulders. Holding her. But she didn't want to be held. 'But that doesn't stop me taking you out just once, does it?'

Maybe not normally, but it's not in my psyche to sleep

with someone unless some small corner of my heart has whispered that it could be for ever and I can't play the "maybe for ever" game right now. 'What's the point in one date? Look I'm sorry, last night was fun, but that's all it was.' She shrugged, and tried to ignore the way his fingers had tightened on her shoulders and a tiny voice in her head was screaming "liar". 'Can't we just say goodbye like grown-ups?' Because I can't paint and make promises, I just can't. I can't. She forced herself to take a half step back, even though her body was saying it was the wrong direction.

'That could be a problem.'

Nope, she could do it; what did he think he was, totally irresistible? OK, he was nearly, but not totally. 'I don't think so.'

'Oh Hayley.' He had the faintest quirk to that strong, straight mouth that made her want to stretch up and kiss him. 'You really don't know who I am, do you?'

Why the hell should she know who he was? He was Tom, the guy whose eyes had seemed to follow her round the gallery, the one man in the room who'd drawn her to him like a magnet. The light in the dark that she couldn't resist because she'd known it was impossible. Fate.

'Thomas Holah?'

Nope, try again, mate. Maybe he was famous and she'd missed it – some B-list actor. Let's face it, she didn't even recognise the A-list stars if she bumped into them, so what chance did he stand? Though with looks like that she was so sure she'd have instantly known him if she'd seen him before.

'I'm your client, Miss Tring, the mystery guy who's commissioned the paintings? I'm the man you've just told me is the most important person in the world right now.'

'No, that was that man with you, that guy who –'

'That guy was my PR man, Hayley, the guy who insisted I take a look at your work.'

Shit. That was bad. That messed things up on a major, out of this world scale. How could she keep her emotions to herself if she had to work for a man who she had an insatiable urge to lick and nuzzle all over?

Chapter Two

'CALLING PLANET TOM, ANYONE there?'

Tom glanced up with a guilty start and met the quizzical stare of his PA. 'Sorry, I was ...'

'Miles away, I'd say, and I guess you're not going to explain where?' She cocked one eyebrow and waited, still holding out a pile of papers patiently. Hanging on with reluctance when he tried to take them.

'Correct, Annie, you know me so well.'

'You can be so boring, Thomas Holah.'

'Boring by name and boring by nature.' He grinned. 'And don't you forget it, Annie Marshall.' Annie had worked for him since he'd started up, and she knew practically everything there was to know about him, but this was one time he wasn't talking. 'You're worse than my mother, you know.'

'I know, 'cos you can't talk to her about your woman issues.'

'Annie!'

She grinned knowingly. 'Oh, come on.'

'I don't have woman issues, I never have woman issues.'

'First time for everything, sunshine.' She winked. 'You really look like you could do with a decent night's sleep, you know. Too much bed and not enough sleep?'

He would have liked to scowl and send her away with a sarcastic comment, but she was right. 'Out.' He'd not had enough sleep, and for all the wrong reasons. Like thinking, and trying to work out why, for the first time he could remember, he wanted a woman and she didn't want him.

The door clicked shut quietly behind his PA and he leant back in the leather chair, swivelling round to look over London from his prime office spot. He didn't have woman issues, ever – or he thought he didn't, until one in particular had bounced into his life. One that had kept him awake last night, having the kind of dirty thoughts that shouldn't be allowed.

Hayley Tring had stopped him in his tracks. He hadn't needed Simon to point her out as the artist because he hadn't cared who she was. She just glowed, centre stage, and he hadn't been able to look at anyone else all night. Everywhere he looked she'd been on the periphery of his vision, a bright beacon of visible energy. Totally different to every woman he'd ever slept with, but totally everything his body wanted the moment he'd seen her.

She was slim, slender to the point of untouchable, and yet he'd wanted to, needed to, reach out and feel her. His fingers itched to glide over those elegant cheekbones, and he wanted to see if the burnished gold skin stretched flawlessly over every tantalising inch of her body. He'd wanted to feel that curtain of silken red hair brush over him, wanted to sweep the heavy fringe to one side so that he could look into the depths of those deep green eyes. And he'd wanted to strip her totally bare and explore every inch of what was underneath.

Which was romantic tosh, seeing as he didn't know her from Adam.

She'd been restrained when they'd been introduced, but just the lightest touch of those cool fingers had sent a rush of blood to his groin. And when he'd bumped into her on the way to the cloakroom he hadn't been able to help himself. She'd practically jumped on him like an excited puppy, and so he'd done what came naturally. And then he'd wanted to do it again.

No woman had ever fallen so magically apart as she came, never cried out his name as though it mattered. Never screamed and begged and laughed and cried and made him wish he'd got the energy to keep going all night.

But there again, no woman had ever thrown him out in the morning, leaving him with throbbing balls and an instant hard-on every time he thought about her. He thought she knew who he was, but that look of horror and the "well, that really is the icing on the cake" comment before she'd practically pushed him out of the door knocked that notion on the head and left him bloody confused. So it certainly hadn't been a gratitude fuck. But the way she'd touched him and wept what looked like real tears made it hard to believe that it had just been a quick shag for her.

He turned back to his desk and stared blankly at his laptop. He'd only agreed to go to the exhibition because he didn't trust Simon to drag his tired image into the 21st century for him. Simon scared him. And art bored him, until he'd seen the paintings and, for the first time ever, actually felt something he couldn't quite pinpoint. Although he could pinpoint exactly what he'd felt when he set eyes on the artist. And it had a lot to do with the current ache in his groin.

Drumming his fingers on the desk wasn't helping either; he stopped abruptly and put his hands behind his head, willing the tension out of his body. Making sure she hung about long enough to produce the pictures he wanted was all about proving to the PR company that he knew his business better than they did, but stopping her shutting him out was more than that. For some reason she'd convinced herself that dating and drawing didn't mix. And he wanted to know why. And he wanted her.

And the fact that she didn't want him made him even more determined. Even if it might be more than a little bit selfish.

The buzz of the intercom made him start guiltily; he was being irrational. She was supposed to be the flighty, arty one, wasn't she? He was the sane, sensible, boring one who dealt in black and white. The one who put business first and knew when a deal was worth chasing.

'A Ms Tring just called, Tom.'

'Put her through.' Every part of him stiffened, jumped to attention, even though he'd given his dick strict orders to stay out of this.

'She isn't on the line.'

'Well, why the hell not? Get her back on.'

'She said she didn't want to talk to you, she was just returning your call and wanted to leave a message.'

Shit. 'What do you mean she doesn't want to talk to me?' She really did think she could just walk away, just dump the commission ...

'She said ...' There was a shuffle of papers as though Annie was checking her notes, but there was a smile in her voice which said she knew exactly what she was doing to him. 'She said she's available for lunch to discuss business at 12.30, The Gallery.'

'The Gallery? As in the art gallery?'

'The Gallery is what she said. I told her you had a prior engagement, which –'

'You told her what?'

'That you had a prior engagement –' Annie's calm tones washed over him '– but I'd be able to rearrange.

And I have done.'

This was ridiculous. He was being ridiculous.

'I knew it was woman trouble.' The warm sound of satisfaction ran through her voice. 'Who is she?'

'Just an artist I've commissioned.'

'Just? She's made you very jumpy.'

'It's business, it was Simon's idea.'

'Oh, sure. Do you want to know when I've rearranged your other lunchtime appointment for?'

'I'm sure you've put it in the diary.' At least common sense had won over and she was prepared to do the paintings, which meant that, like it or not, she'd have to talk to him. And he'd be able to see her again.

'I have. And Tom?'

He forced the image of her naked body out of his head reluctantly. 'Yes, Annie?'

'Don't forget to sign these letters before you go, will you?' The tinkling laugh was cut off as she flicked the intercom switch. She'd baited him for years about his inability to commit, teased him remorselessly when he'd refused to let a woman become more important to him than his work, and now it seemed that womanly sixth sense was working overtime.

He was in a suit, which, if anything, was sexier than the jeans he'd worn to the exhibition. It made him look smooth, sleek, and dangerous, which wasn't what Hayley wanted at all. She wanted boring and ordinary. Grey.

'I'm glad you changed your mind.' He grinned in a boyish way that made her want to wrap her arms round him, and bury her head in his chest and ... Bugger.

'I haven't changed my mind.' She ran her tongue over suddenly dry lips and tried to avoid his eyes, which meant staring at his broad chest, and down to his hard, lean thighs, and big, warm hands. Boy, they'd been warm; she could still feel the heat he'd generated in her as he'd stroked his way over every inch. Stop it; she had to stop it. 'I, we, I need to talk to you about the paintings.' She paused as Maisie, one of the assistants at the gallery, carefully unwrapped a plate of sandwiches. Waited the lifetime it took to slowly peel the clingfilm off, to painstakingly straighten the individual triangles. They were sandwiches, for God's sake. It didn't matter. 'If you still want me to do them, that is.'

'Talk away, then.' He sat down, smiled a brief thank you at Maisie and ignored the makeshift lunch. He was making her nervous the way he was just sitting, staring at her in that curious searching way he had. Bloody nervous. And hot. All over.

'I wish you'd stop looking at me.' He grinned. 'You're putting me off.'

'I know.' The grin broadened, reaching his eyes until they crinkled slightly at the corners. 'You're gorgeous when you get agitated, you know.'

'Bugger.' Bugger, bugger, bugger. So much for being calm and professional. Concentrate. Talk business. This was business, and all she had to do was keep it that way. Talk. And stop looking at him, do not look at him.

She picked up one of the sandwiches and studied it, peeled a corner up. 'Cress? Do people still put cress on sandwiches? Look I'm sorry, but it's just I can't ...' The words froze as he leant forward, pulled the sandwich from her fingers, and dropped it back onto the platter.

'I still want you to paint for me, Hayley, and I still want to take you out.' She couldn't avoid those eyes any longer, and he seemed to be seeing straight into her soul. It wasn't the words but the way he said them that sent goosebumps down her arms. 'I don't know anything about art, but I know everything about doing what you believe in.'

'You could find someone else.' Please.

'I've already found you.'

'If I'm going to paint then it's got to be ...' He raised an eyebrow, which, for some reason, made her even more nervous.

'All business, no pleasure?'

'Something like that. I can't paint if we're, well, you know, involved,'

'We can just shag, no involvement?' His eyes were crinkling at the corners even if he was keeping his face straight.

'It's not funny, Tom.'

'I'm not laughing.'

'Why did you come to the exhibition? I mean, you're not really into art, are you?'

'Whoa, quick change of direction.' He was giving her that lopsided smile again. 'Is it that obvious? The me and art thing?' He leant back a bit, which at least took him further away from her twitchy fingers. 'I guess it is from that silence. Well, I was told you were the perfect antidote to my boring, dull existence. Or rather, your paintings would be. I've been told –' he lowered his voice conspiratorially '– I need livening up, a bit of colour in my grey life, would you believe it?'

'You were lively enough the other night.' Bugger. She shouldn't have said that; it slipped out in normal Hayley fashion a nanosecond before her brain caught up and told her it was a bad idea.

'See, it's working already. OK, OK.' He held up a hand at the look she threw him. 'But I don't get why we can't have fun while you're doing the work. Surely a bit of fun can't do any harm, can it?'

'But it's not always fun and when it's not fun I can't paint happy and I paint happy best. I'm shit at painting tortured.' There, she'd said it, and from the look on his face she could imagine the confusion rattling round his brain. But she'd learned her lesson from Chris; too many high and lows, too little time to paint. And then the low. The real deep-down low when painting a black canvas would have been all she was capable of. With a splash of stupid regrets.

'I don't want tortured, I can do that on my own.' He had picked up one of the sandwiches, was turning it round and studying it, and for the first time she could remember he wasn't looking at her. 'I want fun and happy. Your paintings kind of light up a room, you know. Something about them just kind of grabbed me.' He sounded slightly surprised, as though it was the first time he'd thought about it. 'Though that's a crap way of saying it. But my life is all about work and winning, very dry.' His voice had a strange edge and he still wasn't looking at her, then he took a bite of the sandwich and pulled a face. 'Bit like these.'

Hayley laughed at his expression and something caught in her chest.

'That was a bit of a speech, wasn't it?' He dropped the rest of the sandwich back down. 'We could keep it light?'

'No.'

'Good friends rather than lovers?'

'No.' She fought a losing battle with the smile that was trying to find a way out. 'I need time, my own space.'

'Fuck buddies?'

'Tom!' Laughter bubbled up in her throat.

'Well, I thought we fitted together quite well. Shame to waste it.'

She squirmed, trying not to remember just how well

they'd fitted together, and failing. 'Stop it.'

'So you'll do your stuff as long as I keep my hands to myself, is that what you're saying?'

Oh, if only it were that simple. 'Shall we just see how it goes?' The words she was trying not to say jumped out of her mouth before she could stop them.

'Sounds like a plan to me.' He grinned. 'Celebratory snog?'

God, why was she agreeing to this? What part of her brain thought it was a good idea? 'Who exactly said you were grey and boring?'

'Oh, my mother, sister, PA, you name it – oh, and of course Simon, my wonderful PR guru, who is trying his best to give me a makeover. I'm officially Mr Boring; I never do anything without a plan, you know. I could ruin your life.'

Which is what I'm afraid of. 'Oh, I'm sure you're not that bad.'

'These sandwiches are, though. Can't we go and grab a proper lunch, please?'

'No snogging.'

He sighed. 'God, you're a hard woman, Hayley. OK, no snogging.'

'You can tell me what you want from me –' She'd done it again, that look on his face said it all. 'What you want me to paint.'

'Then after that, can I tell you what I really want from you?' He laughed; a full, deep laugh that echoed deep inside her, making her stomach clench and her pussy twitch. Maybe they could just have fun. Maybe she could do that, enjoy the moment and not want more, not get involved. Or maybe not.

'Sod off.' She grinned. 'Lunch. That's what I want, I'm starving and you, my dear rich benefactor, can pay.'

And when he swatted her rear as they headed for the door, it was nice, and friendly. And moreish. And made her think she'd need to stock up on very long-lasting batteries for her vibrator if she was going to survive this.

He wasn't grey and he wasn't boring. But she already knew that.

'You choose.' He smiled at her over the menu.

'Me? How am I supposed to know what you want?'

'Men do it all the time.'

'True. But it always seemed a bit daft to me.'

'Guess.' His mouth twitched. 'And I'll make you eat what I don't like.'

He'd picked the perfect place, even if he didn't want to pick the food. She loved tapas, quick mouthfuls of fresh flavour, each one a different explosion on her taste buds. 'How did you know I'd like it here?'

'I guessed. Go on, pick, I trust you. I thought you were hungry.'

'Sure?' A grin twitched at her mouth; she liked spice, she liked variety, and she guessed from the way he'd shagged her that he might be the same. But who knew? So she went the full hog from sweet crab to spicy pimiento, from garlic to ginger, and everything in between. At least he wouldn't want to kiss her after that lot.

'You look like a naughty schoolgirl.' His eyes had darkened. 'Which might not be a good thing from your point of view. You've not got a uniform still hidden away at the back of your wardrobe?' He really was going to test every last bit of her self-control. 'I take it from that look that I'm just supposed to eat and stop talking?'

He ate it, all of it, including the big chilli that was decoration, which he stuck in his mouth whole.

'You're changing colour, you know,' she observed. He

was so moreish, even if he was turning a funny shade.

'Not grey and boring?' He choked on the words, tears streaming from his eyes, which made him kind of hard to resist.

'Pink, as in lobster pink.' She really shouldn't laugh at him. Really. He was just too easy to – well, to connect with. 'Is that how you want your paintings?'

'I want –' He topped up their wine glasses and dabbed at his eyes with his napkin. 'Fuck, I want to be able to breathe again.' She watched transfixed as he took a long swig of water, could sense it rippling its way down his throat. She could kiss her way down that neck; feel that Adam's apple move under her tongue. 'I want you. In the paintings, I mean. I want colour and life and spontaneity and fun, everything my boring predictable life hasn't got. Is that stupid?'

'No, it's perfect.' Christ, why did she have to sound so mouse-like and feeble, and emotional? But every painting she did was her, which was why she had to stay free – why she needed every bit of herself, her emotions, there under her own control. Not trapped, not damaged, not high and low and totally fucked up every which way. 'And, erm, how big?'

'Massive, mind-blowing.' He threw his arms wide, stretching his shirt button to just short of popping, then seemed to realise he was being uncharacteristically demonstrative and gave her a sheepish grin. 'I want them to be the first thing people see, and I want everyone to stop in their tracks and think our company must be the most exciting thing since sliced bread.'

'Sliced bread isn't very exciting.'

'Since chilli-enhanced tapas?'

'Better. If you're – well, a boring ... What are you, exactly?'

'I run a service and solutions company, IT solutions, you know ...' He paused and took a sip of wine.

She loved that hint of perfect crisp white cuff under the dark jacket when he stretched his arm, the way he ...

'You don't know, do you?'

'Sorry?' What had he said? Something about servicing, IT?

'I'm a man in a suit who sits in meetings all day telling other people in suits how they can run their companies better.'

'Oh that, piece of cake, then.' The way he'd loosened his tie just a little bit uncovered that kissable V of brown skin at the base of his neck, that little dip where he tasted all salty.

'I'm boring you.'

No, not at all, keep talking. She took a sip of the perfectly chilled wine and ice trickled its way down her own throat. 'No, you're not. It's just I was thinking – well, how come you look like you spend all day in the gym? I mean, shouldn't you be all flabby from those business lunches?' Not toned and perfect, not fit with the type of stamina that left a girl a quivering, useless jelly.

'I do all kinds of stuff in my spare time.' He shrugged. 'I'm an adrenalin junkie, I like to push myself to the limit.'

'So you're not boring.' She knew he wasn't.

'I do it in a boring, predictable way. You know, rock climbing, freefalling, abseiling – stuff like that.'

'Rock climbing, freefalling? You call that boring?' She'd gone all squeaky. 'Predictable?' Very squeaky. She took another gulp of wine.

'Well, what's the worst that can happen?'

'You die?' He was mad. Worse than mad, he was crazy, suicidal.

He shrugged again. 'Well, the odds are against it. I'm fit, been trained properly, buy the best equipment, and I'm in control of my body.'

Maybe she should forget all her stupid "being in control of her emotions" crap. He could fall out of a plane tomorrow, fall off a cliff, be gone for ever before she'd had a chance to – get to know him. She shuffled uncomfortably on her seat, and all this talk about danger was winding her up, turning her on.

Stop it, Hayley. She clamped her thighs together, which made it worse. Studied her fork so that she wasn't studying him. 'Go through my website and tell me which are your favourite paintings, and why. Give me a list of words, thoughts, things, people, emotions, anything that's important to you, and I'll come up with some ideas. Unless you already know what you want me to do?'

'I don't need ideas. Just paint what you think I want; you probably know better than I do.' The lightest touch of his finger on the back of her hand made her glance up and meet his gaze. 'Come into the office tomorrow and I'll show you round and tell you where the paintings are going to go.'

'You already know?' Pulling her hand away would be rude; leaving it there was just ramping up the heat in her body from smoulder to furnace.

'I always know exactly what I want and where I want it.' Her stomach gave a little lurch, because he looked like he fully intended to get it, and sometime soon she'd forget that the word "no" even existed.

Chapter Three

OK, SHE KNEW IT and he knew it. She had to go ahead with the commission. How could she say no to the man, or the work? On the sensible side, it would be professional suicide to turn the work down because there were absolutely no secrets in the art world. And she'd always been sensible. Everyone knew he'd been at the gallery, everyone knew that he'd chosen her work to adorn his prestigious offices, so where was the choice in that?

But there was more to it than that; there was a very unsensible side. The side that involved him being on her mind 24/7. She could smell him on her sheets, hear him in her head, and feel him in her body. She wanted, needed to see him again. Something deep inside was nagging away like an old woman and telling her that if she said no she'd be sidestepping a man she shouldn't. She'd never know, never be sure of what might have been; she'd be having dreams, or more likely nightmares, about him and his hands, his searching eyes, his mouth, and that wicked tongue for years to come. She just knew it, which was a bit of a bummer. A lot of a bummer.

She caught sight of her reflection in the full-length mirror and her mouth curled into a secret smile as she rolled on the sheerest pair of barely black stockings she had. Oh yeah, who was she kidding, telling herself she didn't care? That she didn't want him to want her as much as she wanted him? She was as excited as a kid at Christmas about seeing him again, but shit, all she wanted was to know that the warning voice in her head was wrong, that having fun with a guy who woke up every nerve ending in her body wasn't going to end in a car crash of an affair that left her in brittle shards. Like it had with Chris.

She ran her hand over her knee, over the cool smoothness of her thigh. He should be touching her, his warmth caressing, sliding up her barely covered calf, up until he met the slightest tempting flash of pale skin, up until the heat of his hand bled through her silk knickers.

A slight tinge of colour spread along her cheekbones as she surveyed herself, moving her hands up to cup her small, rounded silk and lace-covered breasts. He'd said they were the perfect handful and she'd never really thought about it like that before. Her grin widened and a small shiver spread over her skin; they'd been more like the perfect mouthful. Her nipples started to tighten into peaks and she brushed both thumbs over them, sending a buzz straight to her clit. Maybe she could get by on just fantasising about him until after she'd done the paintings; the memory of his tongue snaking over her breasts, of his mouth closing around her soft flesh.

She closed her eyes, savouring the moment of anticipation as she ran her hand down her stomach, glided effortlessly under the silk, her finger instantly homing in on her swollen clit. The lightest pressure sent a shiver through her hot, swollen flesh as she circled, tipping her head back, imagining his mouth on her throat, travelling down her body, the languorous swirl of his tongue on her swollen nub. His lips closing around her, gently tugging before he sucked, hard.

In her imagination it was his fingers that sank deep

inside her slick channel, and she gasped as her pussy clenched urgently, cried out as the intrusion tipped her over the edge, her hand instantly damp with her juices as her swollen flesh pulsed greedily around her.

The soft moan filled the room and she paused, waiting for the last of her orgasm to drift away before opening her eyes and staring at her reflection. Green eyes glowed back, dark with arousal, her cheekbones dusted with pink. Slowly, she lifted her damp fingers to her lips, ran her tongue over them, sucked gently, shuddering at the heady smell, the sweet taste that flooded her senses.

She could do it, she really could. She didn't need his touch, his demands and complications. She could let her mind do the work, let the crystal sharp memory of what he'd done to her satisfy the cravings he'd triggered in her body. She could keep it light.

She picked up the emerald green silk dress from the arm of the chair, lifted her arms so that it slithered sensually down over her body, and then slipped her feet into the black stilettos. The dress looked almost demure; almost knee length, with a neckline that sat just high enough above her cleavage to be business-like. But demure wasn't how it made her feel. She grinned as the sensual material wrapped itself round her body, the skirt floating around her legs so that the slightest breeze would send it thigh-ward.

She pulled her hair into a ponytail, and then stood back to study the end result. Most of her time was spent in scruffs, clothes that got covered in paint smudges and charcoal, so it was nice to dress up and feel sexy. And it was just for her, not for him. Definitely not because she wanted to see those golden eyes go dark with lust. Nope, it was to make her feel good, confident. In charge of the situation. And herself.

Her reflection grinned back wickedly as she shifted her hips so that the silk caressed her inner thighs. Demure with a hint of dirty. Well, maybe more than a hint; her face was still flushed and she had a feeling he'd know exactly what she'd been up to. To hell with it; sex had never been off the agenda, just relationships and getting so lost in someone else that you forget who you are. Like was fine, and sex with people she liked was fine, and bringing herself to orgasm thinking about people she liked was fine. So it was fine, all fine.

And she was perfectly capable of facing him and not thinking about watching him strip naked, and she could ignore that cute dimple and lopsided smile that made her want to kiss him. And she wouldn't tremble inside when his skin met hers. She'd just find out where he wanted the paintings, work out what he wanted. And then she'd get on and make it happen. The work bit. Not the lust bit. Definitely not the lust bit. Not yet.

'Tom, Miss Tring is here.'

'Oh, call me Hayley, please.' She was smiling at Annie, and Annie was smiling back, and all he could do was stare, probably slightly open-mouthed, as his cock battled to see what it was missing out on. Shit, how the hell was he going to stick to those best intentions if she insisted on dressing like she needed undressing?

'Hi there, Tom.' She smiled, the picture of innocence, almost. Took a step closer and he could have sworn the bloody dress tightened round her hips, caressing her mound in the way his hands should be doing.

'You look stunning.' He couldn't disguise the rough edge in his voice as he stepped past her and pushed the door shut on a hovering Annie. She even smelled of sex. 'I need to get my hands on that gorgeous body of yours.'

He could have sworn she was trying not to giggle. 'We had a deal, Mr Holah.' There was a hint of a frown as she smoothed her hands over her hips. 'Changed your mind already?'

'We said we'd see how it went, Miss Tring. But I think you might actually kill me in the process.' God, he so wanted to get his hand on those stockings, to push her dress up to her waist and uncover the golden glow of her thighs. 'You do look amazing, Hayley.' His voice was cracking. Maybe he just needed to get this over with fast, stress his brain so that his body didn't have chance to take over. Yell out to his cock that his entire blood supply was urgently needed up top.

Or beg her to kneel down in front of him and suck him off.

'What are you thinking about?' Her eyes had narrowed and he wasn't sure if they were green or hazel any more.

'I was being selfish.'

'Oh.' She flushed, which didn't help his self-control one iota. 'Do you think you better show me where you want the paintings?' Her words had a throaty catch to them, but enough of an edge to tell him that she was doing her best to ignore the buzz between them. OK, she wasn't going to suck him off. Not yet.

'Well, I want one in here.' He waved at the wall to the right of his desk. 'Simon says I need a personal touch, a bit of me, whatever the hell that means.' Bollocks to that; didn't he just want a touch of colour? 'And then I want something with the wow factor in the lobby. I'm after impact.'

'Aren't you always?' The note of almost innocence was what got him, mixed with naughtiness. She really deserved a good spanking ... He groaned inwardly as an image he really didn't want flooded his mind and made his cock harder than ever.

'Stop it, unless you want me to ignore all the rules and sort you out over my big desk. Come on, let me take you down, as in to the lobby.' She raised one elegant eyebrow, then led the way past a goggle-eyed Annie, who looked like she had prime seat for the spectacle of the century. He glared, which got a bigger grin. God, the women were out to get him today, which was probably his own fault. For deciding he had to win a battle he should have never started. It wasn't good for her, it wasn't good for him. Maybe he was being cruel, insisting she did the work for him. Whatever she was frightened of might be for good reason. What if by insisting she do this he really did destroy her creativity? What if she couldn't paint? And all because of him. One shag. But it wasn't about one shag, was it? He wanted more; the only bit he didn't know was exactly how much more.

Hell. He shoved his hands deeper into his pockets; the way she was sashaying those hips in front of him made every step a challenge. He really, really had to lift that skirt up to her waist, bend her over his desk, and shag her until she screamed out his name and begged for more.

'So you want it there?'

'No, there.' He dragged his gaze from her bum and pointed.

'There? Really, right where everyone can see it?' Her eyes opened wider.

'That's the idea.' He would wrap that ponytail around his hand; hold her tight while he thrust so hard that his balls slapped against her bum.

'You're sure?'

Then he would pull the hairclip out, free her hair, slide her off the desk so that she knelt in front of him, the tendrils of her hair flicking against his stomach as she wrapped those perfect red lips around his cock. 'You're really sure, Tom?'

'Oh yes, I'm really sure.'

Hayley gazed at the wall. It was perfect. Nearly as perfect as his erection. She'd been trying desperately not to look at the way his cock had grown harder by the minute, the way it was disrupting the perfect cut of his trousers, but her gaze just kept slipping back to it. The orgasm she'd had before she'd dressed had only made her more desperate and now she just knew she was wet, sopping wet. Do you want to show me what you want in your office? That was all it would take.

He was looking at her intently, his gold eyes glittering, and her heart quickened. Her nipples tightened as he stepped closer; the back of his hand brushed down the side of her face, his fingers tightened around her chin. 'You are so fucking adorable.' Then he kissed her. On the nose. On the flaming nose. Like she was his favourite niece or something. 'Got enough of a feel for the place?' She nodded, her heart thumping as though it was about to break out. 'Good.' He grinned. 'Let me know if you need anything else.'

I need you to kiss me, hard, now. 'That's it?' That's it? She could scream. Or stomp her foot. Or back him up against the wall and kiss him. Or go home and see if her heart went back to its normal pace and if she still wanted to paint. 'I'll go, then, and make a start.' And he just bloody nodded again when all she wanted was him to tear the dress from her shoulders, rip the lace bra away from her breasts, and suck them until her whole body throbbed and ached. Well, it wasn't quite all she wanted. She wanted his mouth on her pussy, his tongue lapping the length of her, and his teeth teasing at her clit until she was writhing in a mix of agony and ecstasy. And instead it was just her jaw that was aching from clenching her teeth. 'Fine.' She spun on her heel, and for a second the world wobbled, which screwed up on the sexy and sophisticated front.

'Hayley?' Oh yeah, he was teasing, right? She half turned back. 'I'll call you later.'

His tone was soft, so soft she could have sworn he wasn't sure he was doing the right thing. And the line of his suit pretty much confirmed it.

The door of the stairwell closed decisively behind him and she stood for a moment in the office lobby. It was perfect. Even the frustration racing through every inch of her couldn't change that. This was something she wanted to do, needed to do. It was the perfect showcase for her work.

The building was old, but with high ceilings and huge windows that filtered the light perfectly. And the wall he'd chosen was facing the right way. It would never be lit by the strongest, most destructive sunlight, but whenever there was daylight it would catch some. Her bright colours would shine from the gloom at each end of the day and glow when they were bathed by light. Rather than one big canvas, she could break it up. She sat down on the visitor seat and stared. Nine square panels – no, three long panels. Three panels with small gaps between, flowing from light to dark in opposition to the natural light. Rich old colours to blend in with the architecture, but with abstract, more modern shapes that would make people pause, make them question what they were looking at. So they could make the image their own.

She fished her phone from her bag and took a couple of photos, then stood up and smoothed her dress over her hips. She needed to get home and sketch, let the ideas in her brain translate through her fingers before she lost the sense of the place.

It didn't take long to cross town, a short walk that, on some days, she would have relished. But today she hardly noticed. Colour and form were swirling through her mind, changing and blending into the perfect picture, and before she knew it she was automatically slotting her key into the door and hurrying up the stairs to the attic room that she used as a studio.

Her easel was always set up, a huge sketch pad spread on the floor, paints, charcoal strewn around, and she kicked off her shoes and settled on the floor, oblivious to the fact that she was still wearing her dress. The dress she wore when she wanted to feel in control, the dress that made her confident because she knew she looked good in it. The dress she had worn to test out her own and Tom's nerve. He'd risen to the challenge and been the perfect gentleman, but left an ache that told her she was the loser. But it hardly mattered now. Wow. She dropped the pencil onto the floor. She'd seen him, she'd lusted after him and yet she was here, with ideas, and she wasn't afraid of losing them. So maybe it wasn't Chris all over again.

She'd thought that feeling like she had today would have left her a nervous wreck; sitting, chewing her nails, wondering what was going to happen next. If they'd see each other again, if she'd get more involved than she wanted to, if she'd rush headlong into an affair that would leave her battered and bruised. And useless.

But it wasn't like that. A strange feeling that was almost contentment cocooned her from the inside out. She felt – well, she felt ... Happy was a stupid word. But it fit. She picked up a charcoal stick and absentmindedly started to draw swirling lines on the sheet of paper, then split it down with three vertical slashes. Yup, she was happy.

God knew how long she sat there, scribbling and planning until she was left sitting cross-legged in her silky soft emerald dress surrounded by a sea of black and white. The abrupt ring jarred her from her trance and, for a moment, she wasn't sure what it was. Shit, phone. Where? She leant back, shifted frantically through the sheets of paper, trying to ignore the pins and needles in her feet. Bugger, not there. Bag, it must be in her bag; damn her feet really had gone numb. She rubbed frantically as she crawled over to the easel and fished the buzzing mobile out of her bag.

'What are you wearing?'

'What?'

'Have you got changed?'

His soft tone drew her back into the world of want. 'No.' Since when had she been able to say one word in a way that made her sound like some wanton hussy? She forgot all about rubbing her feet.

'Good, because I'm imagining you still looking just as you were when you left me. Where are you?'

'At home Tom.' She hesitated. Her studio was private, her innermost mind kept just for herself. 'In the attic, my studio. Thinking …'

'Thinking?'

'Just thinking, sketching.' She stretched out on the floor, rolled onto her back, and looked up at the darkening sky through the roof light.

'I've been thinking too. About you. I haven't stopped thinking since you went.'

'Oh.'

'I've been thinking about that silk dress and what might be underneath it.'

'Oh.' She lifted one leg, pointing her toe skywards, and the fabric slithered down, uncovering her thigh.

'I need to slide my hand up over those black stockings, all the way up until I get to that soft, warm patch of your inner thigh; I love your inner thighs.'

She ran her hand down from her knee, towards her panties; panties that she knew were already damp just from hearing his voice.

'What are your knickers like, Hayley?'

'Black, silk, soft.' She ran her hand in a circle over her mound, every sensation prickling through straight to her skin, and his groan sent a shiver over her stomach.

'You're touching them, aren't you? Touch yourself, Hayley, tell me if you're wet.'

She swallowed hard, slipped a finger in under the smooth fabric, and all she could do was whimper as the damp warmth bathed her. She was so swollen, open and ready, and he'd hardly said a word. Which was fine, perfectly fine, really.

'You've got your fingers in, haven't you?' The sound of him unzipping echoed in her ear and she gulped, imagining his hard cock in his hand as she slid her fingers in deeper. 'Slide them in for me. I want to hear you, 'cos all I can think about is pushing my fingers into that wet pussy, pounding in until you're sopping wet, and then I need to lick you. I want to bury my face between your thighs and lap at your juices.' She moaned and curled her fingers, rubbing against the uneven surface of her swollen G-spot. 'I want to suck your clit, Hayley, until you press yourself hard against my face and scream for more.'

She was close; she pushed her hand in deeper, closing her eyes so that she could hear him palming his cock, imagine him pounding her with one hand while his other was jerking away. He was thrusting harder into her, faster, pulling at his swollen cock, and then he was coming, creamy come spurting over her, and she was coming too, shoving her hips higher as her cunt grasped at his hand, the orgasm shooting through her, her thighs tightening around her hand as she gasped for breath, her body rocking from side to side.

'Oh Hayley.'

Oh Hayley indeed. She opened her eyes and looked up at the dark sky. He hadn't even asked if she'd come, if it was good. He knew. Just like she knew he had from the way his breathing had raced, from the catch in his voice.

'I wish I was there with you.'

'So do I.' She'd said it. The world hadn't caved in.

'I'll call you tomorrow.'

'Good.' Well, no batteries required now. 'Tom, do you think …?'

'Don't even think about thinking. Night, Hayley.'

He disconnected and she held the phone tight to her ear for a little bit longer. Stared up at the inky sky.

'Goodnight, Tom.'

Chapter Four

SHE HALF EXPECTED HER legs to tangle with his when she stretched and spread herself across the bed, but they didn't. There was just a wide expanse of cold, empty sheets. Sleeping through the alarm was something she hadn't done for ages, but the aching lull of her orgasm was still lying heavy in her body and she guessed it was raging happy hormones that left her light-headed.

So that was what phone sex could do for you, which was a revelation because it had been better than quite a bit of the "real-life, both in the same bed" type of sex she'd had. Which would make it a bit boring when she had to go back to relying on silicone and batteries. Stupid girl. She sighed. Why the hell was she worrying about the end? This was going to be an in the moment thing, if it was going to be anything at all.

She swung her legs off the bed, and headed for the shower. She'd wash every thought of him out of her body, out of her mind, and then she'd think about the paintings. Paintings that were for him, of him.

A strong jet of water shot straight out of the power shower, hitting the tense spot between her shoulder blades. The spot he'd massaged the other night. OK. She closed her eyes; he obviously wasn't going to wash away that easily, so she might as well go with the flow.

She turned and the jet of water streamed over her breasts, down her stomach, as she soaped her body, stroking her hands over every inch of herself. Making love in the shower had always seemed wrong; showers were for getting clean, not getting down and dirty. But right now she wanted him here, could imagine his warm mouth on her breasts, his tongue teasing her nipples before he pulled her tight against him. His mouth hard on hers as his tongue delved into her mouth, skated over her teeth in a way that made her shiver, his hands firm on her bum, holding her close against him so that his hard cock nestled between her damp thighs.

She didn't need him inside her right now; she just wanted his body against hers, wrapped round her, holding her close. It would be just enough to taste him, to have her fingers wound into her hair as the water streamed down over both of them. To run her tongue down his neck, to taste that salty spot at the bottom, for that smell of lust, lemon, and cedar to flood her senses.

She snapped off the water and wrung her hair out, grabbing a towel from the rail. Coffee. That was what she needed.

Her sketches from last night were strewn haphazardly across the floor, but they were good. She cradled the warm coffee mug in her hands. They captured that hint of old, of nostalgia, mixed with the vibrancy of new, of life today. A touch more than warm, just the right side of hot. She grinned. What she needed to do today was get a feel for the painting that he wanted in his office, the piece of him. How did you hint at a man with a background of restraint and corporate life, a man who simmered with power and control? Not grey and boring. Sheesh, how he could think of himself as grey and boring? He was all restless energy, coiled inside suited respectability. Yes, his office was a bit masculine and business-like, but the man himself was all edge, ready for the next challenge. Like leaping out of planes.

A shiver ran through her, sending goosebumps along her arms. Just thinking about falling from the skies, free, made her stomach unfurl as anticipation spiralled through her body. As a teenager she'd ridden horses; galloping flat out had always sent an almost sexual thrill through her, anticipation, elation, fear. She wasn't sure what did it, but was that what he felt when he jumped off cliffs, out of planes? That sense of being on the edge, not quite knowing; it sent a knot of desire straight to her stomach.

The mug went down with a clatter. She wanted to capture him, that mixture of thrill and responsibility, of challenge and monotony. She had to capture him. Or rather the essence of him, because she really didn't want him. Really.

Hayley picked up a piece of charcoal and started to sketch absentmindedly. A perfect eye formed under her fingers; dark, intense. Him, looking at her as though he could uncover every little secret, every hidden bit, every hope and fear. Her fingers moved automatically, drawing rough lines, the square jaw, the cleft in the middle of his chin that made him somehow confident, sure of himself. His mouth danced across the paper, slightly lopsided, with that quirk at the corner that said he didn't take himself too seriously, and then his straight, slightly flared nose. She darkened round his nostrils. He was a tiger. He had the strong, defined features, the same confidence and bluntness, but with the soft edge that made you want to reach out. Slowly, she broadened his features, darkened the lines, until power and control took over, until the man became beast, beautiful beast.

She tossed the pad to one side and flopped back onto the floor. She was supposed to be coming up with an idea for his painting, not drawing some fantasy creature. Not thinking about him.

She rested her head on her hands, stretched out flat on the wooden floor, and gazed up through the skylight at the odd white cloud drifting across the perfect blue. Shit, even with her eyes open she could see him, feel him, smell him. Imagine running her hand over his strong arm so she could feel every sinew, every muscle beneath her fingertips. Every part of him was a contradiction; hard and soft, gentle and strong, rough and smooth, all melded perfectly into a swirling mix.

She'd do rocky cliffs. Yes, that was him: danger, pushing to the edge with bright sky; bright figures abseiling against the dark, jagged danger. She could imagine the faint tremble in his muscles, the total control as he went over the edge. The way he'd looked when he'd been poised above her; total concentration, when he'd held himself, when he'd given her that brief moment in time to say no before thrusting deep inside her.

She could imagine those strong fingers finding a hold in the rocks, gripping the ropes, firm, slightly roughened fingers that had traced a path up her thigh, that had rubbed her with a mix of gentle sensitivity and harsh mastery. Fingers that seemed to know exactly where to search, exactly where she needed them.

Hayley sat up quickly, trying to shake the image from her head, and briefly saw stars. That bloody man might not be giving her lows but he'd totally invaded her brain, and her body. She should so totally not be thinking about him; well, not in the way she was. She just needed to concentrate on certain defining elements, the bits she needed. That was all.

She'd sketch a frigging cliff; surely she could do that without his rock-hard pecs flooding her brain? The blank sheet of paper stared back at her. It was easy; she was a trained artist. It wasn't about him, just about hard and soft, control and beauty, the harshest, most defined aspect of the landscape wrapped in the forgiving colours of life and emotion. The contrasting aspects of nature that his business and personal life mirrored.

Hayley concentrated, using her understanding of form to mark in the initial shapes. She could add the life and emotion when she painted; this was just about getting an idea into shape. Form. Her teeth worried at the inside of her cheek. It wasn't flowing like the other sketches had, but it would do. She'd make it work.

She dropped the charcoal stick with relief as her mobile gave a beep. OK, she wasn't supposed to just take any excuse to stop, she should work through this, but what the heck.

Is my favourite artist free for lunch? x

Her heart gave a kind of undisciplined flip and she gripped the phone tighter. She didn't want to be fighting a grin just because he'd sent a text, because that meant she wanted to see him. Thinking about him all the time was bad enough, but just one text and she was an infatuated 16-year-old all over again, which was bad. Especially as she'd never really been infatuated as a teenager; oh boy, no, she'd waited until she was old enough to know better. This was supposed to be a business arrangement; this was supposed to be friends and maybe a bit more. Not OMG I'm having palpitations because you texted me. And you put a kiss.

No, sorry.

Answering texts was one thing, abandoning ship altogether was seriously asking for trouble. Keep it light, keep it light, that's all you have to do.

Doing some work for a v important man.

And it's really not working because I wish he was here. The man who's taken up residence in my head, the man who is making my body rebel against my brain.

I'm sure he doesn't mind waiting.

The easiest thing in the world would be to stop. Let him interrupt. But that was where it all started going wrong, when the man became more important than her work, when her priorities slowly started to shift.

Later.

The mobile vibrated like an angry wasp, which was what it did when the ring tone was turned off. She was tempted to just ignore it. So she did. It stopped buzzing, so she had to pick it up, like you do. When you just have to know. No message, nothing. So she should be happy, mission accomplished, but she wasn't. Shit, she should ring him back. She pressed the missed calls, stared at his number. She wanted him, but she didn't. He scared her, she scared herself. And ... Shit.

The doorbell rang. Which at least gave her a reason to stop staring at her mobile. It should have been a delivery man. Should have been. But it was him. Stood on her doorstep, leaning on the door jamb holding pastries and coffee.

'Can't have you wasting away.' He grinned and shouldered his way in, his six foot against her five two.

'Tom, I'm trying ...'

'To pretend I don't exist?' He had dumped his bounty and settled on one of the kitchen stools.

'To work. You know, do my stuff? And I can't and you're making it worse.'

'I'm not trying to tie you down, Hayley.' He was opening the pastries, keeping his tone conversational and light, but he still frightened her, because she wanted to move closer. 'But I want you so much that it's giving me a pain in the gut.' He glanced in her direction then, and all she could do was open her mouth and close it again. 'You know I want you to paint.'

'I need my own space, Tom, I told you that.'

'I know you do, but it isn't just that, is it? What are you so scared of?'

'I'm not scared.'

'You are. Why don't you just start at the beginning?'

She looked at him. The beginning. 'OK. Once upon a time ...'

He smiled and pushed a pastry and coffee across the breakfast bar. 'There was this man?'

'There was this man.' She pulled a piece of the pastry off, chewed it slowly.

'Who you fell in love with?' His voice was soft, and this time the question had an edge to it.

'Who I fell in love with.' He held her fast with his gaze. No way out. The pastry dropped from her fingers. 'Who I thought I'd fallen in love with.'

'And?' His hand was next to hers, the barest of contact that asked for more.

'His name was Chris. He was good-looking, and popular, and clever and ...' She paused, and suddenly knew what it was that she'd been searching for. 'And I felt like I wanted to spend every spare second of my time with him.'

'So you stopped painting?'

'Not at first, not completely, but I wanted to be with him. At first it was just in the evenings because he'd moved in, and the weekends, and then he'd have some wild idea for a day out and we'd drop everything.'

'Nice if you can do that.' The dry edge made her glance up, and he shrugged sheepishly.

'He was a musician.'

'Ah.'

She tried to ignore the slight hint of censure. 'He liked having me there when he rehearsed, there when he played, and I wanted to be there because I wanted to share everything I could with him. So the painting kind of got neglected for a while.'

'Ah.'

'What's that ah for?'

'Seems a bit of a one-way street, that's all. Wasn't he proud of your painting, didn't he want you to do it?'

'Well, yes, I suppose.' Well, no, we were too busy doing other stuff, his stuff. 'Well, I don't know, I wasn't really earning anything so I suppose he just thought of it more as a hobby. But don't have a go at him. It was my fault, not his.'

'Sure.' Which didn't sound like he meant it.

'I paint when I want to, and I didn't want to, OK? I'd start something and then – well, something would happen and I'd feel down and stop, and we'd make up and I'd be on a high. It was always kind of extremes with Chris; he was in the clouds or depressed, and he took me with him. Anyway, we had one row too many and it finally clicked that Chris didn't want a happy ever after. He thrived on pain and unhappiness and –' she slowly tore the pastry into small bits '– it just made me sad, I guess.' She shrugged. 'And he kept flirting with all the bimbos who followed him around which made me mad, which is –' she paused for a moment, remembering '– partly why he did it, I think. So we split. And that should have been that. I was relieved, I suppose, but I still just couldn't paint ...'

'Because you only paint happy.'

Something tugged at her insides. 'Yup, I only paint happy, and I just felt kind of empty. I didn't want to fill the gap he'd left and run round laughing like everything was suddenly OK again.'

'I won't make you sad.' He was all serious and even closer, and she wanted to believe him, she really did.

'You won't mean to make me sad. But I don't think it's just about happy and sad. I think I just need to feel free. If I'm all wound up with someone it just doesn't happen. I can't just shut it away in a box.'

'So you're all wound up with me?' His voice was soft as he traced one finger slowly down her cheek.

She swallowed hard, trying to resist. 'I didn't say that.' But I'm getting close, so close.

'Maybe it's just if you're all wound up with the wrong kind of person it's a problem? Have you ever thought of that?'

And how do I try that without risking fucking it all up again and losing everything? 'I don't know.'

'I'd never try and trap you.' He stood up, moved round until he was standing next to her. He was so close now that the heat of his body was warming her, and he'd kiss her soon and she'd kiss him back …

'This is about me, not you. It's all in my mad, artistic head.'

'I like you just the way you are, Hayley.' Her nipples prickled against her T-shirt as he ran his thumb over her lips. 'Including your artistic head.'

'You're already in my head, stopping me thinking straight.'

'Then paint what's in your head.'

'You really don't want me to do that.' What was in her head most of the time was pure porn when it came to him.

His lips were on her forehead, on her nose, and the swelling want in her breasts was trickling down lower, pooling in the base of her stomach. 'Paint what's in your heart.' He was nibbling her bottom lip, and each tug was shooting a message straight between her warming thighs. 'I promise I won't try and trap you –' his tongue skated along her teeth, making her shiver '– if you promise not to shut me out.' The last words drifted into her mouth as his lips came down gently on hers in the softest, most sensual kiss she could ever imagine. 'We can just have fun, enjoy each other.' He cradled her face in his hands as he teased her, tempted her into opening her lips wider, into exploring his mouth with her tongue, and as the taste of his lust started to play with her senses her whole body melted against him. His hair was soft under her fingers, soft and silky, and as she wound her fingers in deeper he groaned. She pressed her body harder against his, and he wrapped his arms round her and pulled her in tight, his kiss deepening but still so gentle that it made her ache with want.

He pulled back slightly and kissed her on the nose, then traced down it with the lightest touch of his finger. 'You are so damn hard to resist, you know.'

OK, she shouldn't have glanced down at his crotch, but she couldn't help it. She wanted him desperately, every bit of her screaming out for him.

'Don't even think about it, Hayley.' She could have sworn there was a tremble in his voice. 'Go back and do your silly artistic head stuff and I'll see you later. I just came because you sounded like you needed someone. But I'm taking you out tomorrow whether you like it or not, so be ready at 8 a.m.'

'Out, where?'

'Heaven.' He grinned. How he disentangled himself so quick and shot down the stairs she didn't know. She was still tingling and hoping as the heavy clunk of the door shutting behind him echoed through the house.

Chapter Five

'ARE YOU OK IN there?' Tom leant in closer to the firmly shut door and swore inwardly at the sound of her unzipping the jumpsuit, hoping she wasn't taking it off and looking for an escape route. But at least she wasn't puking up, which he'd seen more than one person do.

'I'm fine, go away.'

There was the slightest edge to her voice that he hoped was excitement, but his stomach dipped as he considered the other alternative. Fear. But he'd thought she'd be up for it, was so sure her eyes had shone when he'd told her where they were heading. Maybe it was the gleam of tears. Fuck. Just because he enjoyed jumping out of planes didn't mean she would. 'You don't have to go through with it.'

'I want to. Now will you just bugger off?' She sounded cross, not scared.

'You're not shut in there because you're scared and planning a runner, then?'

'I'm shut in here because I'm bloody excited.' He heard, felt, the clunk of her head against the door on the other side. 'I'm wound up, excited ...' There was a crack in her voice, a definite crack. 'I just need ...' She'd gone kind of distant. If she wasn't being sick and she wasn't using the toilet ... A rush of blood headed straight to Tom's groin. 'I just need ...'

'A wank?' He hadn't meant to say it quite that loud.

'Shh, someone will hear. And that's a horrible word.' She seemed to be struggling to get the words out, which meant ... He groaned and felt his cock stiffen.

'There's no one else here. You've got your fingers in your damp pussy, haven't you?'

'No.' She gasped, and not the kind of gasp you normally hear from a toilet cubicle.

'You're wet, aren't you, and you're rubbing your clit, rubbing round and round.' The smallest of moans seeped through the door. 'God, I wish I had my fingers inside you, filling you, stretching you.' He cupped his hand round his cock. 'Don't you wish I was filling you with this big, hard cock –' her stifled gasp caught him right in the balls '– thrusting deep inside until you scream out.' A small sound midway between a moan and a gasp sent an ache right to the base of his stomach, a familiar sound that had been locked in his mind since they'd met at The Gallery, a sound he wanted to hear so much more of, the sound of Hayley coming.

He took a steadying breath. 'Want a hand with your zip?'

'Go away while I have a wee.'

He laughed. 'And what if I want to listen to that too?'

'You're weird, now bugger off.' But she was smiling; there was a tease of it in her voice.

He grinned and headed back into the morning sun, and hoped his hard-on went before they jumped, or he might do himself a serious injury.

'Will you stand still a sec?'

'I'm trying.' She was jiggling from foot to foot in anticipation and grinning, which made him want to kiss her. Except kissing her was seriously bad news for his heart rate, and the direction of his blood flow. He snapped the harness into place and checked the straps.

'You're supposed to be scared; you're supposed to be clinging to your strong, manly protector.'

'My what?'

'Your hero, the one who's going to look after you.'

'Oh yeah, you mean that gorgeous, hunky pilot.'

'You, girl, are asking for a spanking.' Her eyes shone and the grin widened. He shouldn't have said that, he really shouldn't have said that. He fought the urge to smile, to kiss her, to drag her back to the restroom. 'Me, right? I'm your hero.'

'Really?' Her eyes widened. 'Well, if you're sure.'

'I'm sure. Now you remember everything we went through?' He tugged at her straps again. God, he was more nervous than she was.

'Yup, I think I need another wee.'

'Oh no you don't, I'm not standing here thinking about your fingers in your pussy again just before we get in the plane.'

'A wee, I said a wee.' A trace of pink etched its way along her cheekbones, and for the first time she looked slightly worried. So he let himself kiss her, just once, just lightly on her soft lips, ignoring the invitation as they gently parted.

'Come on, you're going to love this.' Tom couldn't help but smile as he helped her in. This was the best part, as the plane taxied, took off, and headed up into the sky. It didn't matter how many times he did it, how many times he went for the perfect jump.

The thrum of the engines reverberated through him. This was the part when the anticipation built, the thrill started to creep through his body, and from the way her hand was tightening in his it was getting to her too.

'We'll go at 15,000 feet, OK?' She gave a small nod, a

whisper of a smile as he clipped her harness to his. 'Look.' He wrapped one arm round her, pointed with the other over towards the horizon, and in that moment he felt the sigh of satisfaction that ran through her, that moment when wonder overtook fear, when she relaxed her slight body against his. The grip of her hands eased slightly on her harness straps, colour edging back into her knuckles.

And then they were out, into the blue and her body formed the perfect position without him saying a word, her head lifted as they went into freefall and became part of the sky.

They floated, hung above the world, and only the buffeting of the air against his face told him that they were moving, told him that any second now he'd have to release the canopy and snap the perfect moment. You only get one minute, he'd told her, one perfect minute at most, and he pushed to get as close to it as he could before they were jerked to a halt as control took over from freedom.

'That was …' Hayley struggled for a word as she curled her fingers into the damp grass. 'Incredible.' There was a snap as he unclipped her harness from his and she made to get up, but he stopped her, rolled her over as he leant back so that she lay on top of him in the long grass.

'You're incredible.' She could live on that warm as chocolate voice, that intent look in his tawny eyes.

'Thank you.' He pulled her down tighter against him and her voice went to a whisper as his hard lean body pressed into hers. 'For jumping with me, not saying …'

'I want more than that, Hayley.' He pulled her goggles off, threw their helmets to one side. 'I want you.'

'You want to shag me?' She slid herself along his body and he groaned. 'You want to shove that big, hard cock of yours inside me?'

'You're a witch.' His hands cupped her face fiercely, and he lifted his head slightly so that his lips met hers. Firm, hard lips that tasted of mint, of coffee, and of lust. She could sense his restraint, feel the power, and she wanted it. She met his tongue with hers, pushed back harder, and suddenly, with a groan, he let go and was kissing her with a bruising intensity that made her forget she was in a field.

He rolled her over, his hands tugging at the buckles of her harness, tearing at the zip of her overall, and she did the same, fighting with the hard plastic and webbing that was keeping his body from her hands. She was panting by the time she got past enough of the fastening to get his cock in her hand, his hard, bulging cock. She ran her thumb over the silky, velvet tip and he groaned.

'No way, Hayley.' He grabbed her wrist, tugged the jumpsuit free of one of her legs, and then his fingers were pushing her soaked knickers to one side as he moved between her legs, as he teased her for a split second with the head of his cock, and then he was in and she was already pulsing and wrapping her legs round him, yelling out and rocking as her greedy pussy trembled around him.

'Shit, Hayley.' His face was tight, his eyes glazed as he looked down at her, then three hard thrusts and he came, bathing her insides with his warm juices. 'Sorry, I can't believe I did that. I feel like some bloody randy teenager.'

'What?' She couldn't stop the giggle, or the way her pussy tightened around him as she laughed, sending a last sizzle of sensation through her body. His eyes narrowed.

'Carry on laughing and I might start again.'

'Mmm, that would be nice.' Shit, why was her voice that soft? It wasn't her. Then he was looking at her, those tiger eyes burning inches away from hers, and it was as still as it had been that moment before they'd jumped. That second when he'd been there, looking after her, when she'd trusted him enough to go for it and she'd been freefalling. No one holding her, but someone there.

Hell. She shut her eyes. 'Can we do it again?'

'The shag?'

'You have a one-track mind. The jump, Tom, and then, well, maybe the shag.'

'You have a body that deserves a one-track mind.' His tongue traced a hot path along her neck, sending a shiver through her, making her cunt clench around him. He twitched inside her and she pushed her hips up harder against him, grinding her pelvis against his.

'I love your one track-mind.' This was the moment when it went wrong. She froze, hoping it would go away. That she hadn't just said what she knew she had.

'Only my mind, not my body?' His voice was soft, as though he knew, and then he shoved rudely against her, making her laugh. 'I think we should do this plenty of times again if it makes you this horny.' He bit her neck and she squealed.

'That hurt, you bugger. Stop it.'

'Mmm, I think I'll eat you.'

''Cos you've gone too soft to shag me?'

'Cheeky, I can soon alter that. But –' he paused '– I suppose I should report in properly.'

'You buying time, big boy?' She was greedy to have him again, and his grin said he knew, and he was backing off on purpose. But he was growing inside her, his cock twitching, filling her, and she wrapped her legs tighter round him, pulling him close.

'Did you like your bit of heaven, Hayley Tring?' His voice was serious as he looked down at her, his hips gently rocking so that he was touching parts of her inside that she hadn't known existed.

'I loved it, Thomas Holah, but– ' she paused and bit her lip, watching the trace of anxiety creep into his face, shadow his eyes '– it's made me very randy.'

'Which can't be bad.' His lips brushed her neck, her eyes, finally reached her lips with a tenderness that made her whole body ache. 'Not bad at all.' And his mouth took hers with a caress that every taste bud in her mouth seemed to be savouring, and his hips moved slowly, steadily, so that with each long stroke he seemed to touch another part of her. The gentle rocking built up until she closed her eyes, until her tongue stopped dancing against his, and all she knew was the heat building, spreading inside her, and she came in a gentle ripple of want that made tears prick at the back of her eyes.

'And what would you like to do next, Miss Tring?' He pulled her gently to her feet and tugged the zip of her jumpsuit back up, right to the top.

'Paint.'

Chapter Six

SOMETHING ABOUT THAT DAY freefalling with Tom had triggered a need in her to paint, to prove to herself that she could do it. Even if he was there in the background, even if bit by bit every hard block of resolve was melting away and being replaced with need and want and something she really didn't want to put a name to.

The large paintings for his office reception area had taken on a life of their own; all she had to do was imagine, feel, and the colour and form flowed on to the canvas.

Each morning he supplied her with croissants and coffee before heading off to his office, and each evening he'd be there with beer or wine and a wicked, sexy smile that short circuited every bit of common sense. A smile that made something deep inside her clench tighter, and made the battle to get the picture for his office done that much more like fighting heat with fire.

She'd get up in the night and pad barefoot up to her study to rework lines, screwing her eyes shut to try and block out every facet of his face, even though she'd just left him in her bed and the heat of his body still warmed her. Trying to stop the images that crowded her head from leaking on to the canvas and make it all go wrong. And he didn't comment or ask when she was wound up and scratchy, he just pulled her close, wrapping her in a cocoon of two. Which made it worse and better all at once. But now she had to stop. Share.

'So what do you think?' She'd dragged him straight up to the studio, too twitchy to wait, and now he stood in front of the canvases. With maddening deliberation he tugged his tie loose and undid his top button. She could scream, but it probably wouldn't help.

'Those are ...' His gaze never left the pictures as he dropped his jacket onto the chair. 'They're spot on, brilliant.' He grinned and sent a tingle straight down her spine. 'Very clever.'

'You think they're OK?'

'I love them.' He somehow got a step closer and slipped his arm round her waist, hitting the spot that never failed to send a shiver of want though her. 'And I think I ...'

He was too close, looking at her too intently. 'They're not quite finished yet, I just wanted to give you an idea.' She was babbling, but sometimes babbling was good. Sometimes it stopped things you didn't want to hear.

'You are giving me ideas.'

The panic subsided. 'Rude ones, I bet?'

'Rude and very crude.' He turned back to the pictures and a whoosh of relief escaped from her lungs. 'I do really like them; they're kind of fresh and new, but not too much in your face, if you know what I mean.' Relief mixed with emptiness, like she'd turned off the radio before the song had finished.

'I know. That's what I wanted, new but almost traditional. A twist so that you'd start to walk past them and then suddenly realise they were different and you might go back for a second look. I'll finish them properly next week. And this –' She hesitated, as doubt grabbed at her gut. She'd known those pictures were good, she'd known he'd like them, they captured every emotion, every feeling she'd wanted them to. But this was different, this was the one she'd fought with and still wasn't sure if she'd won or lost. The personal touch. 'This is the one for your office.'

It was hard to flip the cover from the canvas that she had a love/hate relationship with, harder still to wait as the silence grew. Hardest of all to look at him, meet the look in his eyes head on. But she could do hard. She always had. Just like the crags in the picture. 'You don't like it, do you?' The grit in her voice fought a losing battle with the hard lump in her throat.

'It's not that I don't like it.'

'Oh, you hate it.'

'That's not fair Hayley, I never said that.' He didn't look happy and he didn't seem to know whether he preferred to look at the picture or her. 'I don't hate it; I don't exactly not like it, even.' He paused. 'It's just ... Well, it's great, for just a picture but ...'

'Not for your picture. Just for some other office, some other place?'

'It's clever, really.' He took a deep breath. 'I can see the "me" bit in it, the boring bits and the danger ...'

'But? You can be honest, you know.' Even though I'd rather you weren't.

'It's not you.' He grimaced, and she knew she'd stiffened and drawn away from him just a tiny bit. She couldn't help it. 'It's just a picture; you know, a great picture, but ...'

'But?' Were they ever going to get anywhere with this, was he going to spit it out and say it sucked?

'But it doesn't do anything for me. It's like all those other pictures that didn't do anything for me until I met you. All those brilliant pieces of art in all those galleries

I've been forced to walk through.' His voice was soft and it hurt, really hurt. Chipped at places it shouldn't have been able to reach. 'I'm sorry, I'm really sorry, but it's just, I don't know, flat?'

Honest, she'd asked for honest and he'd delivered, like he always did. One hundred per cent. 'Flat.' Shit. 'See? I told you this would happen. I knew it.'

'But the other ones are great, they're brilliant, so it can't be –'

'And that one sucks, right? You hate it, I hate it.' She took another step away, shoving her hands into her pockets, trying to ignore the sudden need to throw the damned picture on the floor and stamp on it.

'You can't just blame being with me.' He was looking at her as though she'd gone slightly mad. 'Be reasonable, Hayley.'

'Reasonable? I am being reasonable. Knowing what you want doesn't always make you bloody right, you know. I've been here before. This is the start, this is the point where it all just starts slipping away, and I can't do that to myself again, I can't.' Heat pricked at the back of her eyes. They'd had the sex, the fun and she'd known all along it was wrong, that she couldn't handle it.

'And what about me? You can do it to me? To us?'

'Us? I told you there couldn't be an us, not at the moment, not until I've done this.'

'So you expect me to just accept all the blame? It's my fault, is it?'

'I don't expect anything.' She took another step back, another step further away from the man who wasn't to blame for anything except wanting her as much as she wanted him. 'I only expect stuff from me. I want to do your paintings. I just need space.' The inside of her cheek stung as she bit hard.

'You've had space. Those other paintings are fine, but this one just hasn't worked. Just do it again.'

'Tom.' Why did he have to make this difficult? Why was he so fucking stubborn?

'Since when did space ever work in a relationship?' He'd raised his voice, but then she saw it in his eyes. That point when he knew he'd said the wrong thing even for himself. Since when was this meant to be a relationship? Neither of them had wanted that. 'Fine.'

Shit. She wanted to grab him, kiss him, wanted him to rewind, and instead he was looking like everything she said was right. 'I just need to …'

And she spun round and headed down the stairs.

OK, he was out of his depth; he didn't do begging, and he didn't do getting involved. And he'd just nearly done both. Not that it would have made an iota of difference. Because he'd blown it.

After they'd been freefalling she'd practically locked herself away up here and he'd let her, because she'd been fizzing with a contagious energy that made him want her more every day. Then he'd seen the fear, the resolution as she'd fought it, and he hadn't dared ask. He'd just shared her bed and shared her body, but too many times she'd not been there, locked away as though she was trying to prove something to them both. And he'd been too scared to pry, to prove her right, and risk her walking away. Even though all he'd wanted to do was tell her it was OK, that he wanted to share, not take away. The one time he'd pushed the point, every sinew in her body had seemed to tighten and she'd gone as brittle as an eggshell on him. And he'd let her. Fuck.

So this was her domain, the place he'd only been allowed in briefly before. He leant to one side, flicked open a sketchpad, and the real Hayley jumped back at him. The Hayley that was present in all her pictures except that one she'd done for him.

His gaze travelled over the ones strewn on the floor; sketches in charcoal, rough drafts in colour. They were good, they were her. She didn't need more space, more time without him. He could back off, but he didn't want to. And he really didn't need to. Unless it was just that she wanted him to …

He leant back against the wall and closed his eyes. Maybe she couldn't do that one picture for him because she didn't want to. And now he'd really screwed up; he'd told her she was crap, proved to her that she'd been right all the time. Except she hadn't. And he might not want a relationship, but he didn't want to let go either.

'Hey.'

Like the mystery she was she'd come up the stairs without a sound. Her light scent invaded his senses just as her soft voice tweaked at his conscience. He was being unfair, and whatever the answer to this was he wasn't sure he had it. 'It's OK, you don't have to worry about throwing me out. I'll leave you in peace.' He held both hands up in defeat.

'I'm sorry.'

'It's fine. I'm sorry, I shouldn't have said …'

'That it sucked? But it does, I know it does.'

'But it's my fault.'

'No, no it isn't. That's why I'm sorry.' He opened his eyes, but didn't dare move another muscle as she walked over to him, her bare feet moving soundlessly on the wooden floor.

'It isn't your fault, Tom, it's my fault.'

* * *

Hayley stared at him, sat on her studio floor, surrounded by her sketches, and her throat tightened painfully. *My fault for not believing, my fault for overthinking things.* Running had been the easiest thing to do: running from him, running from herself and all the things that sent her into a state of frozen panic. The picture had never been right, but she'd battled on with it. It was too self-controlled, too careful. She'd been scared to let him into her life; she'd been too scared to let him into her head, into her painting. She'd wanted to capture him, but she hadn't let herself. How could it be a reflection of him if she spent all her time trying to shut him out of her thoughts? 'I'll fix it, Tom.' *And then I'll try and fix us.*

'What do you mean?' He was looking at her warily, his eyes narrowed. 'You'll run away, that's it?'

'No, I've stopped running. Well, I'll try and stop. Just give me a couple of days.' He looked sceptical, and for a moment there was a look of something she couldn't pinpoint, couldn't identify, and then it hit her. Square in what might have been her belly but could well have been a smidgen higher. He looked defeated, and it was so not how he was supposed to look. 'Trust me, can you trust me?' *Like I'm trying to trust you?*

He nodded; pulled himself back up to his feet. 'These are good, brilliant, in fact.' He waved at the sketches.

'I know.'

'You can still –'

'I know.' She took a step forward and kissed him, just to shut him up, try and stop him trying to work it out for her. 'I need to do this for myself.'

'I can help.' Her heart quickened almost painfully in her chest at the gentle look on his face. Storming out of the studio had been childish and she'd only got as far as the bottom stair before she'd known, before it had hit her that she'd spent her whole life using her art as a security blanket, as an excuse for not letting anyone get close.

'No, Tom.'

'You still want me to go?'

'I've got to jump solo this time.' She grinned, and stepped back away from temptation. 'You can come back later.' She shoved her hands into her pockets. 'If you still want to, that is?'

Chapter Seven

Hayley lay back on the studio floor and looked up at the stars, her own bit of heaven. She was knackered, totally bloody knackered, and every bit of her body seemed to ache in its own sweet way, but a gentle buzz of satisfaction was humming through her. The same buzz she had when Tom held her close, after he'd just about shagged her senseless.

What Tom did to her scared her. Shitless. Not the buzz bit, just the "everything else" bit. It had never been about simple highs and lows like she'd had with Chris; the happy or sad, the screaming or sex. It was warm and fuzzy, anticipation and fear mingled in a way that was filling her head and her heart but not tearing her apart. Just all-invading, as though Tom belonged there. Which was definitely bloody scary. And yet somehow she still had space, space to do what she wanted and space to fill with him.

He might not still want her, but she had to stop being a wimp, and face up to the facts. She loved him and all she'd had to do was let him into her head and stop trying to block him out, even if she'd had to throw him out of the house before she could do it.

Once she'd started she couldn't stop. She'd never worked so long on one piece and she hadn't even needed sketches, she'd just painted straight onto the canvas. It was him, her tiger in the night. A tiger that morphed into so many other things, but the essence of him was there, in the centre. Strong. And that was what he was all about, what his business was all about, power and success. She'd captured the smouldering in his eyes that she loved, a golden glow just about to burst into flames, and she'd captured the movement, the mystery, the pent-up drive and energy, the latent power about to be unleashed. The colours were wild, but it was right for him, his business. It was change, challenge, and the pure magnetic force of the man behind it. Anyone who looked would be able to see the eyes, the essence, but not the man. Her man.

Her mobile stuttered into life and she reached an arm out lazily, yawning as she picked up.

'What's the matter?' There was a sharp edge of concern. Shit, she'd made the man paranoid.

'Nothing, I was yawning.'

'You sound strange.'

Something stirred in her core, the warmth starting to spiral in her stomach. 'I am strange; I need you to come over.'

'There's definitely something wrong, Hayley; it's past midnight and you're asking me over.'

'Hey Mr Boring, whoever said everything stops at midnight?' She stretched her toes out, and the tension built in her muscles, sending a fresh tingle to the top of her thighs.

'I'm actually in my car outside, but I didn't like to just knock in case it made you come over all artistic again.'

The grin tugged at her insides and set the butterflies off. 'I think I've done enough coming over all artistic for one day.' She laughed into the pensive silence. 'Well, what are you waiting for? Come up, there's a spare key in the big pot at the side of the door.'

Answering the door would have been normal. But she didn't want to go down; she wanted to wait for him here in this most private part of her world, of her. Wait for him and let the anticipation build in her body.

The door clicked open, shut, the key clattered on the table; his footsteps echoed on the polished wooden floor, and her heart started to pound in her ears.

He stood and stared and the hairs on the back of her neck started to prickle. He didn't like it. He hated it. Fuck.

'Bloody hell, Hayley, that's ... I don't know quite what to ... I --'

'You can't hate it?' She knew she was whispering. He couldn't; it didn't feel wrong, it couldn't be wrong.

'It's amazing. How could I hate it? But I don't get how it's so different, it's ...'

'It's something personal, like you said, a part of you and a part of me. I just couldn't let myself get that close to you before.' Saying this out loud definitely felt dafter than thinking it. But she wanted to try and explain; he deserved it. 'I kept avoiding what was inside me, what I wanted to paint.'

'But when we're in bed ...' He was staring at the painting as though he didn't want to break the bond. 'I feel like I know every bit of you when we make love.' There was a long pause. 'Inside and out.' His voice was softer, but had dropped a tone so that it snaked right under her defences.

'I know.' She swallowed to clear the stupid lump in her throat. 'I was trying to lock that out when I painted so that I didn't screw up. I know it doesn't make sense, but I was trying to pretend I could switch my emotions on and off, I think. Oh shit, I don't know.' They didn't move, standing shoulder to shoulder, and she knew she was teetering so close to the edge that turning back wasn't really an option. 'It's just – well, I started painting when I was 16, to block out all the shit in my life.' Hot tears pricked the back of her eyes and he reached out, threading his fingers through hers, the feel of him merging with the feel of her. 'My mum died, and Dad couldn't cope with his own feelings, let alone stupid teenage girl hormones.'

It was so still in the room, so silent she could have been alone, but for the first time in her life there was someone really there, listening even if he didn't quite understand. 'And I guess it worked.' She took a steadying breath. 'I shut myself off and put all my emotion into my painting and I didn't need anyone's shoulder to cry on. But I guess I started to use it as an excuse, a way of keeping people at a distance.'

'But what about Chris?' His thumb brushed against the back of her hand, small circles that headed straight for her heart.

'I was totally bloody infatuated. Nothing else seemed to matter until I came to my senses. But it scared me that it was so easy to lose control, to forget what was really important to me.' She swallowed again and tried to force everything back inside. 'I nearly lost everything.'

'But you didn't and –' there was the slightest hint of awkward catch in his voice '– you loved him.'

'No, I was just ready to need someone. But – right time, wrong person.'

'And now?' He was close, close enough for the warmth of his body to seep into her skin, for that familiar smell of him to wrap round her.

'I don't want a way out.' He traced a finger down her arm; the shiver trickled into her voice, and she was suddenly scared of what came next. 'It's – erm, what you wanted, then? The picture?'

'You're what I want.' Warm lips found the spot beneath her ear that never failed to send a sigh through her body. 'Even though you drive me a little bit crazier every day.'

'It'll stop you being grey and boring.' She finished on a squeak as his teeth nipped the soft skin just where her neck met her shoulder.

'I forgot what grey was the day I met you, Hayley Tring.' His mouth travelled down over her shoulder, over the soft cotton of her T-shirt, teased at her already hardening nipple. 'I think you're overdressed.'

A shiver of anticipation rippled through her belly as he pulled the T-shirt over her head, the warmth of his palm against her swollen breast sending an urgent message straight to her clit.

'You stripped me to the bare essentials in that picture so I think it's only fair I do the same to you.'

The back of his knuckles scorched her stomach as he slipped his hands under the waistband of her jeans and tugged her closer, until her breasts rubbed against the smooth softness of his shirt and his lips were a breath away. One flick and the button gave way and he pulled the zip down with agonising slowness, until every nerve ending in her body was screaming at him to hurry. She wriggled her hips as he eased the jeans down, impatiently lifting her feet up out of the tangle of denim and knickers, his laugh curdling through her as she staggered. Firm hands on her waist steadied her body but sent every bit of her insides haywire. He was looking at her, so intently that her heart started thundering in her ears and she was sure she'd internally combust if he didn't do something.

'You're mine.' His voice was a rough growl as he unclipped her bra and a shiver ran through her that had nothing to do with being naked and everything to do with the way his gaze was raking greedily over her. 'You're almost too good to touch.'

'Tom!' Shit, he wasn't going to stop now.

'Almost.' His mouth curled with a wickedness that sent her pulse racing into overdrive. 'Ever thought of doing a self-portrait?'

'My cheekbones are too big.'

'No one will be looking at your cheekbones –' The heat of his finger caressed her cheek as he spoke. 'But they're perfect anyway.'

'I'm too skinny, my hipbones …'

'I love your hipbones.' His voice had a rough catch in it as his hand traced a path down her body. One lazy finger circled her belly, drifted out to her hip. 'I love you just as you are. Cheekbones, hipbones, wacky artistic brain …'

'Tom.'

'Shh.'

She gasped as his thumb stroked over her mound, while he gently pushed between her thighs with firm fingers, edging her legs wider apart. 'I want you so much.' His fingers stroked along her slit, probed, opening her, finding their way inside her, and she clutched at his shoulders as her trembling legs threatened to give way. 'I love watching you come.' His fingers were still but his thumb was circling on her clit, setting off the gentle swirl of orgasm inside her. 'Come for me, Hayley.' The heat of his other hand burnt a path down her spine and she moaned as he reached the bottom, as he pressed against the base. Held her tight. 'I've got you, darling.' And he was pressing in deeper, fluttering his fingers, creating sensations she didn't recognise, and she was coming. Spiralling over the top, on the crest of a wave that was shattering, splintering, sending tendrils of aftershock to every part of her body.

She was panting, still seeing stars, when he kissed her, kissed her properly. His mouth claimed hers, and she moaned, rubbing her hips against the rough denim of his jeans as fresh need slammed through her. His tongue explored, flicking over her teeth, circling the tip of her own tongue until finally he started to suck gently, teasing till her clit started to throb again in response. The taste of lust flooded her senses, lust and a need that had her clutching at his hair, his shoulders, matching the demands of his kiss with her own.

'Oh God, Hayley.' His forehead rested against hers, his breathing rough and uneven, matching her own as they both gasped for air.

'I want you, Tom.' She slipped her hand down between them, rubbed her palm along the length of his hard cock, the heat of him burning through the thick denim. He groaned and shut his eyes, helping her as she fumbled with his belt. 'I need you.' She pushed his boxers down just far enough that she could get her hand round him, feel the silken skin, the long, hard length of him.

'Shit.'

Hayley dropped down to her knees and swirled the drop of precome over his glans with her tongue, the musky sweetness and his groan making her desperate for more. Slowly she pushed her mouth down, her lips just wide enough to take his tip, constricting over the broad rim of his cock as she stroked her tongue over his slit. 'Oh fuck.' His grip increased on her hair as she dug her fingers into his bum, as her lips glided down until the taste of him was in the back of her throat. She sucked as she pulled her lips back up the length of his cock, flicking her tongue against his frenulum until he widened his legs, and his balls tightened. And then she took him again, her mouth engulfing as much as she could, swallowing as he nudged the back of her throat. He held her head tight for a moment as her muscles squeezed the tip of him, pushing in a tiny bit deeper, and then he pulled free.

'Come here.' The rough growl in his voice sent a new want through her as he pulled her to her feet and his mouth roughly took hers. 'That's fucking amazing, but –'

'Please.'

'Please what?'

'Make love to me, Tom, I need you inside me.'

'I thought you'd never ask. But –' He moved back slightly and, for a moment, panic hit as cool air replaced the heat of his skin against hers, like it could still all go wrong. After all, she was the butt-naked one, even if his dick was standing free and to attention. 'Not here.' She turned to head for the stairs, but he was too quick; his hands were on her waist, and before she could object he'd picked her up and thrown her over his shoulder. One firm hand came down hard on her buttocks and she yelped. 'I like having you under my control.' He laughed as she pounded on his back with her fists.

'Put me down.'

'All attempts to escape are futile, my darling.'

'Hey.' She kicked her legs, but he just tightened his grip.

'Hey yourself, honey. Any more wriggling and your bum will be glowing pinker than a baboon's arse.'

'You've got such a way with words.'

'And you've got such a gorgeous bum. Shut up, woman.' It was probably the abseiling or rock climbing, or whatever else he did in his spare time, but he seemed to find her weightless as he headed down the stairs. As they hit the bottom step he sank a finger in her pussy and she yelled out at the sudden intrusion, a yell that turned to a moan as he pressed deeper into her, twisting his hand. She was panting as he threw her down on the bed, wrapping her legs round him as he sank down on top of her.

'You've got too many clothes on for a guy who's been stripped bare.'

He gave a wicked grin and lifted her, his large hands almost spanning her waist as he pushed her further across the mattress until her shoulders were balanced on the edge of the bed.

'Hey, I'm going to fall off.'

'I'll never let you fall off.' She should have guessed from the darkening of his eyes, from the pressure of his hands on her waist, but she didn't. Didn't know what he was about to do until his head dipped down between her thighs and his tongue swept a path that left her trembling. He thrust his tongue into her throbbing pussy and pure pleasure rippled through her. She was rocking, sliding off the bed, clutching at the covers as he licked and nibbled, his hair tantalizing the inside of her thighs.

'Tom, for fuck's sake.'

'What? You don't like foreplay? I was going to kiss you all over, suck …'

'Please.' OK, her tone was needy, desperate, begging. But she didn't give a shit.

He lifted his head, hair tousled and golden eyes gleaming, and then, in one easy movement, he stripped his shirt off and stepped on the bottom of his jeans to free his legs. 'You are one demanding woman, you know.' He thrust deep inside, one hard thrust that threatened to send her straight off the bed. Her stomach muscles tightened and she squealed, grabbing hold of him as she slid closer and closer to the edge with each thrust, and everything was constricting, clenching, tumbling and she was coming, hanging on, half suspended. 'Don't worry. I'll never let you go.'

His voice was broken, fractured, and he was throbbing, pulsing inside her, and she let go completely, hitting the peak before spiralling slowly down like a feather floating on the breeze.

She was only dimly aware of him kissing the top of her head, pulling her close so he cradled her with his body. But she heard his words and echoed them with her own.

'I love you.'

And she let her eyes close, knowing he was there right behind her. Wasn't he always?

More great titles in
The Secret Library

Traded Innocence
9781908262028

Silk Stockings
9781908262042

The Thousand and One Nights
9781908262080

The Game
9781908262103

Hungarian Rhapsody
9781908262127

The Thousand and One Nights – Kitti Bernetti

When Breeze Monaghan gets caught red-handed by her millionaire boss she knows she's in trouble. Big time. Because Breeze needs to keep her job more than anything else in the world. Sebastian Dark is used to getting exactly what he wants and now he has a hold over Breeze, he makes her an offer she can't refuse. Like Scheherazade in The 1001 Nights Seb demands that Breeze entertain him to save her skin. Can she employ all her ingenuity and sensuality in order to satisfy him and stop her world crashing about her? Or, like the ruthless businessman he is, will Seb go back on the deal?

Out of Focus – Primula Bond

Eloise Stokes's first professional photography assignment seems to be a straightforward family portrait. But the rich, colourful Epsom family – father Cedric, step-mother Mimi, twin sons Rick and Jake, and sister Honey – are intrigued by her understated talent and she is soon sucked into their wild world. As the initial portrait sitting becomes an extended photo diary of the family over an intense, hot weekend, Eloise gradually blossoms until she is equally happy in front of the lens.

The Highest Bidder – Sommer Marsden

Recent widow Casey Briggs is all about her upcoming charity bachelor auction. She doesn't have time for dating. Her heart isn't strong enough yet. But when one of their bachelors is arrested and she finds herself a hunky guy short, she employs her best friend Annie to find her a new guy pronto.

Enter Nick Murphy – handsome, kind, and not very hard to look at, thank you very much. And he quickly makes her feel things she hasn't felt in a while. A very long while. Casey's not sure if she's ready for it – the whole moving on thing. But as she prepares to auction Nick off, she's discovering that her first hunch was correct – he's damn near priceless.

The Game – Jeff Cott

The Game is the story of Ellie's bid to change from sexy, biddable housewife to sexy dominant goddess.

Ellie and Jake are a happily married couple who play a bedroom game. Having lost the last Game Ellie must start the new one where she left off – bound and gagged on the bed. As she figures out how to tie herself up before Jake's return from work, Ellie remembers the last Game and has ideas for the new one. Jake is immensely strong and loving and has seemingly endless sexual stamina so the chances of Ellie truly gaining control look slim. Although she has won the Game on occasions, she suspects he lets her win just so he can overwhelm her in the next. She has to find a way to break this pattern.

But does she succeed?

One of Us – Antonia Adams

Successful artist Natalie Crane is midway through a summer exhibition with friend and agent Anton when Will Falcon strolls tantalisingly into her life. After a messy divorce, a relationship is not Natalie's priority. Anton takes an immediate dislike to the shaven-headed composer, but Natalie is captivated. He is everything she is not: free, impulsive and seemingly with no thought for the future. He introduces her to Dorset's beautiful coves and stunning countryside and their time together is magical.

Things get complicated when her most famous painting, a nude self-portrait, is stolen and there are no signs of a break-in. When it's time for her return to London, Will doesn't turn up to say goodbye, and she cannot trace him. Anton tells her to forget him, but she cannot. Then she discovers the stakes are much higher than they first appeared.

Taste It – Sommer Marsden

Jill and Cole are competing for the title of *Best Chef*. The spicy, sizzling and heated televised contest fuels a lust in Jill she'd rather keep buried. She can't be staring at the man's muscles ... he's her competition! During a quick cooking throwdown things start to simmer and it becomes harder and harder for Jill to ignore that she's smitten in the kitchen. Cole's suggestive glances and sly smiles aren't helping her any. When fate puts her in his shower and then his chivalrous nature puts her in his borrowed clothes, there's no way to deny the natural heat between them.

Hungarian Rhapsody – Justine Elyot

Ruby had no idea what to expect from her trip to Budapest, but a strange man in her bed on her first night probably wasn't it. Once the mistake is ironed out, though, and introductions made, she finds herself strangely drawn to the handsome Hungarian, despite her vow of holiday celibacy. Does Janos have what it takes to break her resolve and discover the secrets she is hiding, or will she be able to resist his increasingly wild seduction tactics? Against the romantic backdrop of a city made for lovers, personalities clash. They also bump. And grind.

Restraint – Charlotte Stein

Marnie Lewis is certain that one of her friends – handsome but awkward Brandon – hates her guts. The last thing she wants to do is go on a luscious weekend away with him and a few other buddies, to a cabin in the woods. But when she catches Brandon doing something very dirty after a night spent listening to her relate some of her *sexcapades* to everyone, she can't resist pushing his buttons a little harder. He might seem like a prude, but Marnie suspects he likes a little dirty talk. And Marnie has no problems inciting his long dormant desires.

A Sticky Situation – Kay Jaybee

If there is a paving stone to trip over, or a drink to knock over, then Sally Briers will trip over it or spill it. Yet somehow Sally is the successful face of marketing for a major pharmaceutical company; much to the disbelief of her new boss, Cameron James.

Forced to work together on a week-long conference in an Oxford hotel, Sally is dreading spending so much time with arrogant new boy Cameron, whose presence somehow makes her even clumsier than usual.

Cameron, on the other hand, just hopes he'll be able to stay professional, and keep his irrational desire to lick up all the accidentally split food and drink that is permanently to be found down Sally's temptingly curvy body, all to himself.

Silk Stockings – Constance Munday

When Michael Levenstein meets Imogen, an exotic dancer at a Berlin nightclub, a passionate and intense love story develops. Michael becomes obsessed by mysterious Imogen and falls into a world of intense sexual fantasy and desire. But Imogen is determined to protect a personal, dark secret at all costs and because of this she has forbidden herself love.

With Imogen afraid of committing and afraid of losing what she has fought for so desperately, can Michael break down her barriers and discover a solution to his lover's deep dark secret, thus freeing the enigmatic Imogen to truly love him?

The Lord of Summer – Jenna Bright

Banished to the back of beyond, in the middle of a long, hot summer, Gem and Dan Parker find their marriage filling up with secrets. As they work to reopen the Green Man pub, tensions and unacknowledged desires come between them. From their first night, when Gem sees someone watching them make love from the edge of the woods, her fantasies of having two men at once start to grow and consume her. As the temperature rises, she becomes fixated by her imaginings of an impossible, gorgeous, otherworldly man in the forest. A man who could make her dreams come true – and maybe save her marriage.

Off the Shelf – Lucy Felthouse

At 35, travel writer Annalise is fed up with insensitive comments about being left "on the shelf". It's not as if she doesn't *want* a man, but her busy career doesn't leave her much time for relationships. Sexy liaisons with passing acquaintances give Annalise physical satisfaction but she needs more than that. She wants a man who will satisfy her mind as well as her body. But where will she find someone like that?

It seems Annalise may be in luck when a new member of staff starts working in the bookshop at the airport she regularly travels through. Damien appears to tick all the boxes – he's gorgeous, funny and intelligent, and he shares Annalise's love of books and travel.

The trouble is, Damien's shy and Annalise is terrified of rejection. Can they overcome their fears and admit their feelings, or are they doomed to remain on the shelf?

One Long Hot Summer – Elizabeth Coldwell
Lily's looking after her friend, Amanda's, home on the Dorset coast, hoping it will ease her writer's block and help her get over her ex, Alex. What she doesn't expect is that Amanda's 21-year-old son Ryan will arrive at the house, planning to spend the summer surfing and partying – or that he'll have grown up quite so nicely. Ryan's as attracted to her as she is to him – but surely acting on her feelings for a man 14 years her junior is inappropriate? And when Alex makes a sudden reappearance in her life, wanting to get back together, should she follow her head or her heart? How can she resolve this case of summer madness?

Just Another Lady – Penelope Friday
Regency lady Elinor has fallen on hard times. The death of her father and the entail of their house put Elinor and her mother in difficulty; and her mother's illness has brought doctor's bills that they cannot pay. Lucius Crozier was Elinor's childhood friend and adversary; and there has always been a spark of attraction between the pair. Now renowned as a womaniser, he offers a marriage of convenience (for him!) in return for the payment of Elinor's mother's medical bills. Reluctantly, she agrees. But Lucius has made enemies of other gentlemen of the upper echelon by playing fast and loose with their mistresses, and one man is determined to take his revenge through Lucius's new wife ...

Safe Haven – Shanna Germain
Kallie Peters has finally made her dream come true – she's turned the family farm into Safe Haven, an animal sanctuary. But financial woes are pressing in on her, and she's worried that the only way to keep the farm is to allow her rich ex-boyfriend back into her life. When a sexy stranger shows up in her driveway with a wiggling puppy in his arms, she knows it's her chance for a hot rendezvous before she gives up her freedom.
The sex is hot, wild and passionate – the perfect interim before returning to the pressures of real life – but something else is happening between them. Can they find a way to save their dreams, their passions and their hearts, or will they have to say goodbye to all they've come to love?

Xcite Books help make loving better with a wide range of erotic books, eBooks and dating sites.

www.xcitebooks.com
www.xcitebooks.co.uk

Sign-up to our Facebook page for special offers and free gifts!